"So I'd only get hurt if I got involved with you," Cora said.

"Yes. You'd essentially be getting a locked box."

He was being transparent, completely up-front. She was the one who'd set that tone. So it surprised him when she barked out a laugh. "You think you're doing me a favor by staying away!"

He was trying to adhere to the decisions he'd made after that last ugly blowout with Tina. He'd been glad for the peace and balance he'd found since they'd broken up a year ago. But twelve months was a long time to go without a woman... "Essentially."

"Well, you're taking a lot for granted, Mr. Turner. First of all, how do you know I'm going to want you to love me?"

"Experience," he said wryly. "I have yet to encounter the opposite problem."

* * *

SILVER SPRINGS:
Where love changes everything!

Dear Reader,

I'm *so* excited to introduce you to my new Silver Springs series! If you've read much of my work before, you'll probably know I like to change things up. I'm an eclectic reader, which inspires me to be an eclectic writer. I currently write women's fiction (like *The Secrets She Kept* and *The Secret Sister*), suspense (e.g., the Stillwater Trilogy, the Last Stand series or the most recent Evelyn Talbot Chronicles). I've even written four historical romances (that's where I got my start—with a historical titled *Of Noble Birth*). But I always come back to straight-up contemporary romance. It's my home, if you will—where my heart resides. I love building a small-town community, am fascinated by the dynamics that take place in a setting where everyone knows everyone else. How and when strangers can and do impact that type of insular world makes it even more fun. Places like the fictional Gold Country town I created for my Whiskey Creek series—and Dundee, Idaho, the fictional setting of the series before Whiskey Creek—really excite my imagination, because I'd love to live in such a place. So I hope you will enjoy the latest. Like Whiskey Creek, Silver Springs is located in California, where I live, but it's in a very different part of the state, and the characters, and the challenges they face are very different, too.

I love to hear from my readers. I have an active Facebook page, where I interact on almost a daily basis. If you're also on Facebook, please join me there (Facebook.com/brendanovakauthor) and/or visit my website at brendanovak.com, where you can sign up to receive release information, news of signings and other events, my favorite recipes, notice of sales and promotions, and the opportunity to enter various giveaways, etc. There's also a list of all my fifty-plus titles you can download from the website, which will make it easier to follow a certain series or trilogy.

Welcome to Silver Springs!

Brenda Novak

Finding Our Forever

—

Brenda Novak

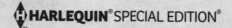
HARLEQUIN®SPECIAL EDITION®

Recycling programs
for this product may
not exist in your area.

ISBN-13: 978-0-373-62338-9

Finding Our Forever

Copyright © 2017 by Brenda Novak

This edition published by arrangement with Harlequin Books S.A.

For questions and comments about the quality of this book, please contact us at CustomerService@Harlequin.com.

Printed in U.S.A.

www.Harlequin.com

New York Times and *USA TODAY* bestselling author **Brenda Novak** is the author of more than fifty books. A five-time RITA® Award nominee, she has won many awards, including the National Readers' Choice Award, the Booksellers' Best Award and the Silver Bullet Award. She also runs Brenda Novak for the Cure, a charity to raise money for diabetes research (her youngest son has this disease). To date, she's raised $2.5 million. For more about Brenda, please visit brendanovak.com.

Books by Brenda Novak

Harlequin Superromance

Sanctuary
Shooting the Moon
A Family by Christmas
Dear Maggie
Baby Business
Snow Baby
Expectations

Dundee, Idaho

A Baby of Her Own
A Family of Her Own
A Husband of Her Own

MIRA Books

Dundee, Idaho

A Home of Her Own
Stranger in Town
Big Girls Don't Cry
The Other Woman
Coulda Been a Cowboy

Whiskey Creek

Discovering You
A Winter Wedding
This Heart of Mine
The Heart of Christmas
Come Home to Me
*Take Me Home for
   Christmas*
Home to Whiskey Creek
When Summer Comes
When Snow Comes
When Lightning Strikes
When We Touch

To all lost/hurt boys.
May you find an Aiyana Turner in your life.

Chapter One

Cora Kelly had never met her birth mother.

The records had been sealed when she was adopted as a newborn twenty-eight years ago. Her adoptive mother didn't even know her birth mother's name, so it wasn't as if Lilly Kelly had ever mentioned it. Cora had had very little to go on. Even with two different attorneys, a website designed to help families reconnect and a private investigator who'd taken her case for free since he was an adoptee himself and did what he could, in his spare time, to help others who'd been through the same thing, it'd taken six long years to glean the information she craved. But here she was, only moments away from coming face-to-face, for the first time since the day she was born, with the woman who'd brought her into this world.

Would she like her mother? Would they resemble each other more in person than in the one picture she'd seen? Would Aiyana Turner somehow recognize her for who she was?

Those questions churned in Cora's mind, making her stomach churn, as well. But one question weighed heavier than the others: Was she making a mistake?

Wiping her palms on her slacks, she told herself to calm down. As far as Aiyana knew, they were only meeting to talk about Cora's new job working as an art instructor at New Horizons Boys Ranch, a boarding school for troubled teens, ages fourteen to eighteen, ninety minutes outside LA. No way would Aiyana have any reason to suspect Cora's true identity. And Cora didn't plan to tell her who she was. Not today. Maybe not ever. That was why she'd sought this job—and accepted it. So she'd have the chance to see what she might be getting into before making that decision.

Hopefully, her mother would be someone she could admire, at least. From what she could tell, Aiyana had done a lot to help teenage boys who acted out, some who'd been orphaned as well as many who hadn't. Her work as executive administrator of the school she'd founded twenty years ago seemed to be her one true love. She'd never been married, and she'd never had any more of her own children. According to a newspaper article honoring Aiyana on the anniversary of the date the boys ranch opened, something the private detective who finally solved the mystery of Aiyana's identity had provided, Aiyana had adopted quite a few of the residents who'd come to the school through the years—eight of them, so far. The oldest, Elijah Turner, was now a man in his early thirties. He helped run New Horizons. Cora knew because he was the person who'd interviewed and then hired her. That was why she hadn't yet met Aiyana. Aiyana had been out of town when Cora came two weeks ago.

"I'm sorry it's taking a few moments. Ms. Turner is on an unexpected but important call." The receptionist, a gray-haired woman who had to be in her sixties, smiled kindly as she imparted this apology. "I can't imagine it'll be much longer."

Hauling in a deep breath, Cora smiled. "It's fine. I don't mind waiting." She *didn't* mind, except that she was beginning to fear she'd have a heart attack right there outside of Aiyana Turner's office. Somehow, she had to stem her anxiety...

"Are you too warm, dear? I can turn down the air..."

She glanced up at the receptionist again—and realized she'd been fanning herself. "Um...no. I'm okay, thanks," she said and dropped her hand.

"It's been hot this summer."

"Yes, it's particularly warm today," Cora said, but it was generally worse where she lived in Burbank. Along with Jill, her best friend, Cora rented a small condo just outside of Hollywood, where her adoptive parents still owned the lovely four-bedroom home where she'd been raised.

She felt a twinge of guilt when she thought of her parents, Brad and Lilly. They'd been good to her, treated her just like her brother, who was two years older and their biological child. They wouldn't be pleased that she'd landed this job if they knew the driving force behind it.

Don't think about that. What they don't know can't hurt them. It would be premature to drag them into this, anyway, since she had no idea where it might go. For all she knew, it wouldn't go anywhere. And maybe that was for the best. Several years ago, when she'd first mentioned that she'd like to find her birth mother, Brad and Lilly had acted shocked and disappointed. They'd taken it personally, didn't understand that they didn't do anything to cause the emptiness inside her and weren't the ones who could fix it. The hole was just there, and Cora felt it would be until she could figure out where she came from, who she was and where she belonged.

She hoped this would help. Her boyfriend—*ex*-boyfriend since she'd broken up with him last month—claimed it was her personal problems that'd destroyed their two-year relationship. He said she needed to let go of her past and move on, that she could be opening Pandora's box.

He could be right. But it was too late to change her plans. She'd already made a yearlong commitment to New Horizons. Today's meeting with Aiyana was merely a formality—an orientation, of sorts. Cora had given notice that she'd be vacating her condo at the end of the month, at which point her friend would get a new roommate and she'd move to Silver Springs, a town of only 5,000 people located slightly east of Santa Barbara.

After spending her whole life in the big city, Cora wasn't sure she'd like living in such a rural area, but if she had to pick a small town, this one wasn't bad. Known for its robust arts community, the renovation of its downtown, its clean water, green energy, recreation and quaint small businesses, there was a lot to recommend it. Life was just slower. Those who didn't grow up here came to retire, raise a family in a "safe place" or enjoy the beauty of the surrounding mountains—

"Ms. Kelly?"

Cora's heart jumped into her throat. The drone of the voice she'd heard coming from the inner office had fallen silent. This was it! The receptionist was about to tell her she could go in…

"Yes?"

"Ms. Turner will see you now."

For a moment, Cora's determination faltered. But when she didn't move, the receptionist—Betty May, according to the placard on her desk—stood expectantly. "It's right through here," she said with a puzzled expression.

Swallowing to ease her dry throat, Cora nodded. "Right. I was just…" *About to run the other way…* Letting her words fall off, since she couldn't readily lay her mind upon a good excuse, she threw back her shoulders and crossed the room to step inside an expansive office with several rows of pictures on the wall—every graduating class of New Horizons.

Those pictures melted into the background as soon as Cora's eyes landed on the diminutive woman with long black hair that fell in a braid down her back. *This* was where she'd gotten the golden color of her skin, Cora thought as she stared. That detail hadn't been quite so apparent in the grainy picture she'd seen with that newspaper article, but her mother appeared to be part Mexican, South American or maybe Native American.

Wasn't that something she should've had a right to know without having to go to all the trouble and expense she did?

Cora had always been conscious of the difference in her skin tone compared to the Kellys. Lilly had blond hair and blue eyes and, like many of her friends, had indulged in a fair amount of Botox and cosmetic surgery. Aiyana, on the other hand, didn't look as though she'd ever altered anything.

"Ms. Kelly, I'm so sorry for making you wait. That call was about another candidate for the school. Considering the mischief he's been in, I figured I should handle it as soon as possible. His poor grandmother, who's raising him, is beside herself."

Cora blinked rapidly, battling a sudden upwelling of emotion. She'd *longed* for this day. And here it was. She was looking at her *mother*.

But she couldn't act strange or she might give herself away. What had Aiyana just said? Something about the wait and the reason for it— "Of course," she managed to respond, dragging what she'd heard out of short-term memory before it could disappear into the ether. "I understand that the welfare of the boys has to come first."

Aiyana's smile as she gestured toward the chair on the other side of her desk suggested she appreciated Cora's response. "Please, take a seat."

Cora could hardly pull her gaze away long enough to sit without missing the chair.

"Eli tells me—"

"Eli?" Cora echoed.

"Elijah," she clarified. "My son."

"Oh right." Aiyana was talking about the incredibly handsome but imposing man who'd interviewed Cora two weeks ago. If only Cora could think clearly, she would've made that connection as instantly as she should have. He'd certainly left an impression.

"He told me you graduated from the University of San Diego with a BA in art education six years ago."

"Yes. I love art, and I love teaching, so…putting the two together seemed like a natural for me."

"You've been working as a substitute since then?"

"That's right. When I first graduated, I was grateful for the flexibility subbing gave me, because I was doing a bit of traveling with my parents. Since then it's been difficult to find a full-time position, given that so many schools are cutting back on their art, music and sports programs."

"I understand. So that's why you answered our ad?"

One of the reasons—though not the most important. Ironically enough, she'd been offered a full-time position for the coming year at the school for which she'd substituted most often, so she'd no longer needed the opportunity. The art teacher at Woodbridge High was retiring and had put in a good word for her. But, to her parents' consternation, Cora had turned it down. Aiyana was *here*. That meant New Horizons offered something no other school could. "Yes."

Aiyana peered at her more closely. "Is something wrong?"

Tears were getting the best of her despite all her efforts to suppress them. "Allergies," Cora explained. "It's that time of year. Fortunately, they don't last long."

"Would you like me to get you a tissue?"

Cora used her finger to remove the tear that was about to roll down her cheek. "No, I'm fine. My eyes are just… a little itchy, that's all."

"Let me know if you change your mind," she said. "I'll get you something if you need it. Meanwhile, I'd like to talk to you about the importance we place on art here at the ranch. Most other schools focus on core subjects, and as an accredited high school, we certainly make that a priority here, too. But it's my feeling that our students cannot excel in those classes—in *anything*—if they're too broken to care or try. I believe in healing those who will be healed by showing them the beauty of life and giving them a healthy form of expression. I guess it would be safe to say that, around here, you aren't merely an extra, the first teacher to go when the budget gets tight. You are our most important teacher, which is why I asked to meet with you before you started in a couple of weeks."

"I admire your philosophy." Cora agreed with it, too. But hearing that *she* was the most important teacher at the ranch was intimidating, since this was her first full-time position.

"I want my boys to be educated," Aiyana continued, "but even more than that, I want them to be whole, to find peace."

"Makes sense to me."

"Good. I should warn you that most have never been introduced to drawing, painting or pottery. They think school has to be boring and hard, which is what makes it so rewarding to introduce them to the fun side of learning. Creative endeavors are one of the best tools we have to ease the pain and anger that's inside so many of them."

"Does that mean all of the students here come from a difficult background?" she asked.

"Quite a few. Some have been abandoned. Some have been abused. Some have behavioral issues that can't be blamed on any of those things."

"You mean like autism."

"We have a few autistic students but only those who are highly functioning. More often it's something else—a chemical imbalance, genetic factors. No one can say for sure. Some brains are just wired differently than others."

"Those boys must be the toughest to reach."

"Sometimes we don't reach them at all. But, that said, we're going to reach all we can."

Cora could easily imagine the rich parents of a boy who had behavioral problems being willing to pay a large sum to enroll him at the ranch. But how could orphans afford such a school? "What about the costs associated with coming here—for those who don't have parents, I mean? Does another member of the family pay for it? Or maybe the state?"

"We get some state assistance, we have private bene-factors and we do two big fund-raisers a year. As much as thirty percent of our students come here without pay-ing a dime. This year, that equates to eighty students. But as long as we can meet our monthly expenses, I'm satis-fied. If we have extra, I'd much rather use it to try to save another boy."

Cora almost felt guilty that she'd be taking a salary. She nearly spoke up to say she could make do with less, but she knew that wasn't the case. In LA, she'd been able to augment her income by waiting tables on the weekends. Chances were, in such a small community, she wouldn't have the opportunity to get a second job. "That's very noble of you."

Aiyana gestured as if she wasn't interested in praise. "I only mention it so that you'll understand what's important to me. It isn't turning a profit—it's making a difference. And I'm looking to work with people who are as invested in the progress of these boys as I am."

"I understand. I'll do my best," Cora said. "But...why have you focused exclusively on helping boys? Why not girls? Or girls *and* boys? Do you have a strong gender preference or—"

"No. Not at all. I didn't want the added responsibility of mixing the two genders, knew it wouldn't be easy to keep them apart," she said with a chuckle. "The boys who come here have enough to worry about without adding that kind of temptation. This is a time for them to focus on getting their lives in order. Hopefully, as a result, they'll make better husbands and fathers later."

"You're saying it was purely a practical decision."

"Absolutely. Someday, on the opposite side of town, I'd like to open a school exclusively for girls, and do essentially the same thing. Now that I have Elijah handling so much around here, that's more of a possibility than ever before. I just haven't geared up for the push it will require."

"I'm sure you'll do equally well with girls." At least now she knew that her mother hadn't given her up because she didn't like girls. Perhaps that'd been a silly thought to begin with, but Cora couldn't help searching for The Reason. Maybe that was all she really needed to know in order to be satisfied…

"We'll see. Now, I've been told you'll be moving into the housing on campus. But have you seen where you'll be living?"

"Not yet. Mr. Turner showed me the school and some other parts of the property, but he didn't offer me the position until after I got home, so we didn't go inside the faculty housing."

"Well, the cottages aren't big, by any stretch of the imagination, but I like being able to include them in the package we offer our teachers. I figure discounted rent might tempt them into staying for a while." She grinned. "Longer than a year."

This comment revealed that Aiyana was well aware of her arrangement with Elijah. "It's a nice benefit."

"You'll find we're more like a family here than what you've most likely experienced in the past," she said with a wink.

A family… Those two words nearly caused Cora to

burst into tears. Aiyana had no idea how literal their connection was.

As Cora followed Aiyana out of the building, she couldn't help thinking back, over all the different ways she'd imagined her mother while growing up. As a drug addict who didn't care about anything except her next hit. As a prostitute eager to rid herself of the child from an unwanted pregnancy. As "the other woman," abandoned by her lover after telling him she was going to have his child. As a businesswoman who refused to allow motherhood to get in the way of her ambition. There were more, but each scenario provided a ready excuse for adoption. She'd never pictured Aiyana like she was—soft-spoken, seemingly wise, well educated, accomplished, stable, kind, loving and devoted to a cause.

Cora had expected that just by meeting her mother so many of her questions would be answered. But she was more baffled than ever. What happened twenty-eight years ago? Why would someone like Aiyana Turner put her only child up for adoption?

Chapter Two

"So...do you like the woman you'll be working for?"

Cora was packing up the kitchen of her condo in Burbank with Lilly when Lilly asked this question. For a second, Cora froze, fearing her adoptive mother had figured out the reason she was moving to Silver Springs. But when Lilly kept wrapping glasses in newspaper and putting them into the box she was filling, it became apparent she was merely making conversation. She *didn't* know—not yet, thank goodness.

"I do." She forced a smile despite the discomfort her deception caused. "She seems really nice." Although Cora had been home for a week, getting ready for her big move, she hadn't been able to quit thinking about Aiyana. She'd spent nearly every extra minute on the internet, doing searches on all of the teachers and many of the students who'd graduated from New Horizons—whatever names she could cull from their website, including a graduate who had turned into a professional football player, one who'd just recently been accused of killing the couple who adopted him when he came to the ranch at fifteen and Elijah Turner, who'd hired her. Only one article had come up on him, but it told a lot. When he was ten years old, he'd been kept in a cage like some animal in the basement of his parents' house, and starved until he was only sixty pounds.

Imagining what he'd been through turned Cora's stomach. What kind of people could do that to one of their own children? And where were those people now? Did he know?

Considering what he'd been through, it was no wonder the man was so guarded, so aloof—and so devoted to Aiyana and New Horizons.

"I can't believe you'll be staying right there on the property," Lilly said.

"The school is about ten miles outside of town, so it'll save me from the daily drive."

"What drive? Ten miles is nothing," Lilly scoffed. "The people in Silver Springs must have no idea how long it takes to go two blocks in LA when the traffic is bad."

"Or they *do* know, and that's why they live there." Cora held up her blender. She made a lot of smoothies and "green" drinks, but her machine was nearly worn-out. Was it worth taking with her—or was it time to get a new one?

Newspaper crinkled as Lilly continued to wrap. "Traffic or no, I could never leave the city."

Brad's office was only a few blocks from their house. He'd been so successful managing other people's money that he could set his own hours. And Lilly did charity work, mostly on nights and weekends. "You two are in the kind of situation that makes it easy to stay. Traffic isn't a huge part of the equation for you."

"Our lives haven't always been so perfect," she said.

Reluctantly, Cora put her blender in the pile for Goodwill. "No. You've worked hard for what you have," she agreed and meant it.

Her mother stopped packing long enough to squeeze her shoulder. "You'll build something, too, honey."

"I hope so." Right now it felt as if Ashton, her brother, was going to be the one to make them proud. Although Lilly and Brad hadn't been too pleased when he left law school to become a movie producer, he already had an indie film out that'd garnered several awards, so they were less critical of his decision than they once were. "From this vantage point, it looks like I have a long way to go."

"It all comes with time."

Cora checked the clock on the wall. Jill, an assistant to a film editor at Universal, would be getting off work any minute. Cora had been hoping to be done by then, so they could meet some other friends for drinks, but there was a lot yet to pack. "Is Ashton going to be able to make it to my goodbye dinner on Sunday?"

"I'm sure he will. Your brother adores you."

"Slightly less than he adores all of the women he's dating," she grumbled.

"That's not true!"

It wasn't *entirely* true, but Cora had been feeling a little neglected by her brother since he'd turned into such a big shot and become so busy.

The packing tape screeched as her mother closed and sealed the box she'd filled. "Does Aiyana Turner offer discounted housing to *all* the teachers at the ranch?"

The scent of the marker Lilly used to label the box "Kitchen—Fragile" rose to Cora's nostrils. "She can't. There's not enough for everyone—just a handful of small cottages on the far side of the property, away from the school and the boys' dorms."

"So who looks after the boys at night?"

"Each floor has a live-in monitor they call a 'big brother' who makes sure the boys go to bed at lights-out, get up for school, study during study time and clean their rooms."

"Are they teachers, too?"

"No. Most work in town during the day. I was told that some even drive to Santa Barbara. It's merely a way to acquire free lodging, kind of like managing an apartment building."

"How does—what's her name, Aiyana Turner?—decide who gets the other housing?"

"Every teacher has the option to add their name to the

waiting list and move in if one becomes available. I just happened to hire on at the right time. The teacher who quit left earlier than planned, and my unit wasn't spoken for—probably because it's so small. It wouldn't be big enough for anyone with kids."

"So where do the other teachers live? In town?"

"I'm assuming they do. Although I suppose some might live in Santa Barbara. It's only about twenty minutes away, not a long commute by our standards."

The packing tape screamed again as her mother built a new box. "But will there be enough of a social life for you in Silver Springs? I mean...if you're living on campus, will you ever get out? How will you meet people?"

"I'll meet the other teachers."

"Who will most likely be older or married."

"I really won't know until I get there."

Lilly straightened and rested her hands on her hips. "There's more to life than work, honey. A year might not sound long right now, but, trust me, it'll seem long if you have no one to do anything with that whole time."

"I can always drive home, visit you guys, Jill, my other friends."

"I hope you come home often. But...what about the man who hired you? Maybe you can get something going with him. Jill told me you said he was hot."

Thank you, Jill. "He *is* hot, but..."

"What does he look like?"

Cora pictured the dark-headed, rather intimidating man who'd shown her around the ranch. He didn't say too much, certainly didn't waste words. But those blue eyes were laser-sharp. They didn't miss a thing. Truth be told, he made her uncomfortable. "Sort of like...a pirate."

Her mother opened another cupboard and started packing the plates. "A pirate? That's a positive association?"

"In this case it is." Mostly… When it came to his physical appearance, anyway.

"How tall is he?"

Cora put her salsa maker, which she'd barely used, in one of the boxes she planned to take with her. If she was going to live in the country, she was going to attend a farmer's market occasionally and make homemade salsa. "*Really* tall. And built."

"He sounds perfect."

"Not perfect exactly." That was what she found most compelling about him that he was a little rough around the edges. "He's got a fairly big scar on his face." She indicated the line of her jaw. "Right here."

"What's that from?"

"I didn't ask." And now that she'd read the article chronicling some of the abuse he'd suffered, she wouldn't. "As far as I know, he's already married."

"Did you see a ring?"

"I didn't look," she said, but that was a lie. She had looked—and seen no ring. She'd been curious about Elijah from the first moment they met. But she'd also been apprehensive about the fact that she'd had an ulterior motive for applying at New Horizons, had known he probably wouldn't appreciate that she wasn't being fully transparent.

Her mother grinned at her. "You should have."

"Matt and I barely broke up, Mom. I'm not ready to start dating again, especially in a place where I don't plan to stay." Besides, she wasn't sure she'd be capable of taking on a man as complex as Elijah. There was no telling what kind of scars his upbringing had created, and she wasn't referring to the one on his face, although that could easily be part of the legacy his parents had left him.

"So you're only staying there a year?" her mother said.

"That's right."

"I can't tell you how happy I am to hear it's temporary." Lilly bent to give her a hug. "I love you, you know."

Cora *did* know. And she was grateful. She could easily have gone to a family who weren't so kind and accepting—a family like Elijah had known. "I love you, too," she said and tried to ignore how selfish she felt for doing what she was doing in spite of the fact it would hurt Lilly if—or when—she found out.

Elijah Turner was brushing down his horse when Aiyana found him. At the sound of her footsteps, he didn't need to turn in order to see who it was. If he didn't come for dinner when she invited him, she tracked him down. She always acted as if she had some official reason, some business question to ask him, but he knew she was simply assuring herself that he was okay. Whenever he complained that he was too old for that kind of coddling, she'd say it didn't matter, that he'd always be her boy.

"How was your ride?" she asked.

He lifted Atsila's foot and used a pick to gently clean his horse's front left hoof. "Relaxing."

"Cora Kelly arrives tomorrow."

"I know."

"Is the cottage ready?"

He moved on to the other front hoof. "Of course."

"Are you ever going to explain that decision to me?"

"What decision?" he said, but he knew what she was going to say before she explained.

"To hire Cora Kelly. You knew, as well as I did, that Gary Seton, from right here in Silver Springs, was waiting for that job to open up."

"I interviewed Gary, too—gave him a chance."

"And…"

"I thought Ms. Kelly was better suited for the position."

"She's pretty."

"That had nothing to do with it."

"Let's say that's true—you're not worried that she might be a distraction to the boys?"

"You're saying I should've discriminated against her because she's attractive?"

She gave his shoulder a little shove. "Stop it."

"You were talking about her looks!"

"Because I wanted to see if you agreed with me."

"That she's pretty? I'd have to be blind not to see that."

"So...do I surmise a bit of interest on your part?"

"None. I'm not the marrying type. You should know that by now."

"I'd like grandkids at some point."

"You have plenty of other sons to give you grandkids."

She sighed as if he was being purposely stubborn, "Fine. Obviously, you don't like talking about this subject."

He didn't argue. There were moments he wondered if he truly wanted to be alone for the rest of his life. But he also saw nothing to be gained from allowing his happiness to hang on the love or will of another person.

"You missed dinner tonight," his mother said.

"You said to come by if I was hungry."

"You should've been hungry. It's nearly eight."

"We've talked about this before," he responded. "I'm too old for you to worry about."

"You'll *never* be too old for me to worry about. And you know why? It's called caring."

His problem was that he had the tendency to care too much, to be *too* intense. "I'm fine." He started on Atsila's fourth and final hoof. "I'll grab a bite while I'm in town tonight."

She leaned against the fence post. "Whoa, don't tell me you're leaving the ranch for a social outing. You don't do that very often."

He gave her a look that let her know he didn't appreciate the sarcasm.

Unperturbed, she smiled. "Your dark looks don't frighten me the way they do everyone else."

"They should."

"Why? I know you love me, even if you rarely say it."

"What good are words?" His parents used to claim they loved him, but they only loved themselves and the twisted joy they received from tormenting him. "Words are empty, meaningless."

"Hopefully, someday, you'll regain your trust."

He winked at her. "Don't hold your breath. But... I am very grateful for everything you've done for me. I hope you know that."

"Stop!" She started to walk away.

"What?" he called after her.

"That wasn't a leading statement. I'm not looking for your gratitude."

She wasn't comfortable with it, either. "You want me to fall in love."

"I want you to be *able* to fall in love. I want to see you lose your heart—and not be afraid to let it go. Then I can rest easy, knowing you're completely fulfilled."

"*You* never married," he pointed out, but she offered the usual lame excuse.

"Because I'm married to this place."

Knowing that was all he'd ever get out of her on the subject, he studied her retreating figure. "Yeah, well, so am I."

Chapter Three

Cora was using her Bluetooth to talk to Jill when she passed through the wrought iron arch at the opening of the school, her car packed full of her belongings. "I'm here," she announced as she wound slowly around to where she'd be living.

"That didn't take long. What time did you leave again?"

She'd gone in to hug her friend goodbye, but Jill, dead asleep, had mumbled something about missing Cora, promised to call and dropped back onto the pillows. "Six."

"That's not even two hours ago."

"See? I'm not that far away." Although…it almost seemed as if she'd moved to another planet; Silver Springs was nothing like LA.

"I should've come with you," Jill said.

"How?" Cora asked. "You have to be to work in an hour."

"I could've called in sick. You need someone to be there to help you unpack."

"No, I don't. My mother would've been hurt if she found out I let you come, since I told her I preferred to organize everything on my own." Cora had definitely not wanted Lilly on the ranch. She knew Lilly had never met Aiyana, that the whole adoption had been handled through an agency. According to the documents her private investigator had uncovered, Aiyana had demanded absolute secrecy. But that didn't change Cora's need to keep the two women apart. "I can handle this. The cottage is furnished. And everything I'm bringing fits into my car. It's not as if I'm towing a trailer."

"Still, I'm curious."

"About…"

"The ranch, for one thing. What does it look like?"

"Your basic high school, but with horses and cattle—and some dorms and a machine shop. You'll see it when you come visit me."

"I've been to Ojai but never Silver Springs. How does it compare?"

"The towns are similar, which makes sense. Silver Springs is located in the same valley, has some of the same mission-style architecture. Only they've added a few murals in Silver Springs, like they've done in Exeter."

"Where's Exeter?"

"Central part of the state." Cora pulled into the drive that would be *her* drive for the next year and cut the engine. "My mom took me there once to show me the murals, thought I'd be interested because of my art degree."

"I'm not that big on murals," Jill said. "I've seen some pretty bad ones."

"I've seen a lot that are worse than the ones they have here. The man who painted the one downtown interviewed for my job. I'm still surprised they didn't hire him instead."

"They told you who you were up against?"

"Aiyana and Elijah didn't. When Aiyana showed me the house, she got a call on her cell, leaving me to speak with a neighbor. He said Gary Seton was a friend of his and was really disappointed."

"Why *didn't* they hire him?" Jill asked.

Cora gazed at her bungalow, trying to imagine calling this place home for the next twelve months. "I'm not sure. I would've guessed they'd prefer a local."

"Could it be that Elijah wanted *you* to come to town?"

"No. I didn't get those vibes at all."

"So you think he's married?"

"Not married." There was too much sexual energy surrounding him for him to be in a committed relationship. She could tell he found her attractive—couldn't help finding him attractive, too. A woman would have to be dead not to feel a *little* sizzle when a man like Elijah Turner came around. "Just completely closed off."

"I've seen you approach guys before. You've never been afraid of a challenge."

In this situation, she was. She had a lot to cope with already, didn't need to add a romantic relationship into the mix. Even if she could manage to gain Elijah's attention, she doubted she'd be able to keep it for long. He was too remote. "I'm only here for a year."

"That could prove to be a very *long* year if you plan to remain celibate the whole time," she joked.

"I'll survive." Although…she was already missing certain aspects of her relationship with Matt and, if she was being honest, sex was one of them. "It'd be kind of odd to hit up the man my mother adopted."

"Why? You're not related by blood. You didn't even grow up together. For all intents and purposes, you're part of a different family. You're a Kelly."

Cora dug through her purse, searching for the house key Aiyana had provided her. "On paper."

"More than on paper! You've spent your whole life with the Kellys."

"I was talking from a strictly literal perspective. But that reaction right there is part of my problem."

"What do you mean?"

"Am I being ungrateful simply by wanting to know my birth mother? That tears me up inside, because I *am* grateful. I love my parents dearly."

"It's the same with regular parents. All kids should be grateful and aware of their parents' sacrifice."

"No, it's not the same. There's a sense of entitlement with children who've been kept and raised by their biological parents that doesn't extend to me. Anyway, let's not get caught up in all of that. Bottom line, people would look askance at Elijah and me if we ever admitted to having the same mother."

"You wouldn't admit that, because you don't have the same mother."

Cora groaned to show her frustration. "It's murky. You have to give me that. Regardless, Elijah makes me jealous." So did the other boys Aiyana had accepted into her life. That Aiyana would give Cora away and then take in eight other children left Cora feeling hurt, baffled. "He holds such a prominent place in Aiyana's heart that it makes me wonder why she wanted him and not me."

"We've talked about this."

She climbed out of the vehicle and circled around to grab the suitcase that held her essentials. "You believe she feels the need to fix things—fix people."

"You told me he had a rough childhood. The other boys probably did, too."

Other than her ex-boyfriend, Jill was the only person she'd confided in about her search for her biological mother, her true purpose in coming to Silver Springs, and the background of the man who'd hired her. "No doubt. Elijah's defies imagination. Which only makes me feel worse. When I think of what he's been through, I can't even be jealous without an avalanche of guilt. Considering the emotions he dredges up, I doubt he and I should even be friends."

Jill ignored her uncomfortable laugh. "There were a number of years between the time Aiyana gave you up and adopted him. Her situation must've changed, that's all."

Since both hands were full, Cora used her hip to close the car door. "Maybe that's it."

"You can't always assume the worst."

"It's hard not to. Especially now that I see how func-

tional she is. I mean…if she were a down-on-her-luck prostitute, I could point to that and say, *Makes sense*."

"The fact that she isn't a down-on-her-luck prostitute
is why you're interested in getting to know her. There's
promise there. You believe she might be someone you'd
like to have in your life. That's what scares you. You're
afraid she'll reject you a second time."

Cora had to set her suitcase down to let herself into the
house. "Do you have to be so frank?"

"It's important to know when fear's doing the talking—
to keep things straight in your head."

"It could be a while before *anything*'s straight in my
head—another reason I'd be crazy to get involved with
Elijah, even if he were open to a relationship, which I can
tell he's not."

"Fine. You won't listen to me, anyway. You're too busy
throwing up roadblocks."

Cora wasn't sure she felt any better now that Jill had
conceded. She sort of liked it when Jill was arguing the
other side. Maybe that was because she *did* find it hard
not to think about Elijah. Even though she'd been almost
completely focused on the fact that she'd just found her
birth mother when she had that interview with him, she
couldn't help wondering what was going on behind those
inscrutable eyes… "You were never given up for adoption. You grew up in a big, boisterous, happy family. You
can't relate."

"I've tried to be understanding," Jill said.

"I'm sorry," Cora responded. "I don't know where that
came from. It was uncalled for."

"You're angry. That's where it comes from. And I can
see why. But I'm on *your* side."

Cora opened her mouth to say she believed that, but
before she could formulate the words, she heard a car engine and turned. What she saw wasn't a car; it was a silver

truck. And Elijah was behind the wheel. As he parked in front of her house and jumped out, she felt her pulse leap. "I've got to go," she told Jill.

"Why? What's up?"

She ducked her head so she could speak without being overheard. *"He's here,"* she whispered and clicked the button on her Bluetooth that would disconnect them.

Cora was wearing a silky orange tank with a pair of white linen shorts that showed off her long, tan legs. As Elijah approached with the orientation materials he'd brought, he found those legs to be distracting. But she was a teacher at New Horizons. That meant he couldn't get involved with her, even on a casual basis. Contrary to what his mother seemed to believe—and probably everyone else who was surprised he hadn't hired Gary—he hadn't offered her the position because he had any romantic interest in her. He'd been impressed with her portfolio. Each piece—a sculpture, a painting, a photograph and a piece of pottery—moved him in some way. He liked that she could make *him*, someone who knew very little about art, feel something. Gary Seton's work simply hadn't been the same.

One piece that Cora had brought, the conceptual sculpture of a mother cradling a child, affected him deeply. When she'd unveiled it during their interview, it'd been hard for him not to stop and stare. He'd wanted to keep it—not because he felt *he* needed that kind of love. No one would ever be able to hurt him again. He wanted the boys here at the ranch to experience the safety and security that piece inspired, and he wanted to give them a teacher who could not only depict that emotion but understand it, *feel* it.

Because he knew Gary was disappointed, he hoped he'd made the right choice. Fortunately, the sensitivity he saw in the large brown eyes staring up at him as he drew closer reassured him. She'd wanted the job even worse than

Gary. He wasn't sure why—if she'd needed to get out of whatever situation she was in or was on her last dollar—but he'd been able to feel her eagerness during their interview and he'd responded to that. Maybe this woman would never be able to teach the boys how to create a decent picture or vase, but she should be able to entice them to see the beauty of the world. She *was* part of the beauty of the world. And she seemed open and vulnerable to the point that he almost felt he should warn her to be careful or life would chew her up and spit her out. After what *he'd* experienced, that she could get so far without learning that lesson was a bit of a shock to him.

"Hello," she said.

"I see you made it safely."

"Yes."

He motioned toward the older BMW X3 sitting in the drive. "Can I give you a hand with anything?"

"No, it's okay. I was careful when I packed—didn't make the boxes too heavy. I can grab it."

"Are you sure?"

She nodded, so he handed her the orientation manual he'd brought over. "I doubt you'll care to read *all* of this. Watching paint dry would be more interesting. But there's a table of contents, I figured you could glance through, check out any topics you're curious about and become familiar with how we do things around here."

"I'll take a look at it." When she hugged it to her ample chest, he decided her body was partly what he found so attractive about her. She wasn't as skinny as some of the girls he'd dated. She was curvy—looked soft, comfortable, sexy.

He searched his pocket for the more important part of what he'd come to give her. "Here's a key to the high school, as well as one to the art and ceramics rooms. With school starting next week, you'll be eager to set those up."

"Definitely. Thank you."

"You bet. You received the group email about the staff meeting tonight?"

"I did. That's why I came a few days earlier than I would have otherwise."

"Great. I'll see you there." He started back toward his truck. "Everyone is eager to meet you."

"Mr. Turner?"

"Call me Eli," he said as he turned.

"Okay, Eli it is. Where, exactly, is the meeting tonight? You showed me the library when we toured campus the day I interviewed, but I'm a little turned around at the moment."

He went back and flipped past the syllabus he'd given her to the campus map on the next page. "You're here," he said, and drew a line from her house to the library so she could easily find her way.

"Thank you."

"Sure," he said. But instead of leaving, he went over to her SUV and began unloading the boxes. He just couldn't leave a woman to do that alone, not when it would be so much easier for him.

"Whoa, I can get those," she said, hurrying out to him. "Really."

"There's no need for you to carry all of this stuff by yourself. Just point to where it should go. It'll only take me fifteen minutes."

As promised, in a short time, he had her vehicle completely unloaded.

"Thank you," she said as he put down the last box.

"See you later." His conscience appeased, he started toward his truck.

"Eli?"

He stopped again. "Yes?"

"I—I have a boyfriend. Sort of."

He felt his eyebrows slide up. Then he almost laughed. She was assuming he had an ulterior motive for helping her. "I'm sorry if I gave you the wrong impression," he said. "I was only trying to make your move a little easier."

Her cheeks bloomed red. "Right. Of course you were. I'm sorry."

Cora's face burned as she watched Eli drive off. "What's wrong with you?" she muttered to herself. "Of course he was just trying to help. It's not as if he asked for your number."

That blunder actually said more about her than it did him, she realized. *He* hadn't been anything but circumspect. *She* was the one who'd had a difficult time keeping her eyes off him. She was so aware of him on a sexual level that it was hard to act as if she wasn't, which was odd. She couldn't remember having such a strong reaction to any other man. That was the reason she'd suddenly tried to throw up a barrier. She'd been hoping to give him a reason to look at her differently—or stay away entirely—and wound up making a fool of herself instead.

"I *told* you I didn't need your help," she grumbled to him even though he was gone, and cringed at the prospect of having to face him at the staff meeting in a few hours.

"You had to do that on your first day here, Cora?" she said as she started to unpack.

Her phone dinged to let her know she'd received a text, and she paused to pull it out of her pocket.

Jill. What'd "dark and brooding" have to say?

Dark and brooding. How apropos. But since she was still writhing with embarrassment, Cora didn't want to talk about Eli, so she scowled at the clock. Aren't you at work?

You know I am. I was talking to you while driving here.

I don't want to get you in trouble for being on the phone. I'll call you later.

Is that a dodge?

Yes. But as long as her friend was willing to risk getting caught on a personal call at work, Cora figured she might as well break the news. He said he's not interested in me.

What? Seriously?

Seriously.

But...you just got there.

Cora shoved a hand through her hair as she recalled his startled expression. Yeah, it came up quick. Thanks to her...

How? He couldn't have come by just to let you know he's not interested.

Again Cora hesitated, but when she didn't respond her friend sent her a question mark, so she typed, I brought it up.

At that point, texting fell by the wayside. Jill called to make her explain the whole thing.

"Oh jeez," she said when Cora was done. "I should never have let you go there without me. I could tell you were rattled, nervous."

"I'll get my feet underneath me. I'm just...not myself at the moment. The prospect of rubbing elbows with my birth mother has me...floundering a bit. I was expecting *that* to be difficult, but when I started this whole thing, I was *not* expecting my mother to have adopted a son who..."

"Who..." Jill pressed.

She pictured the muscles that bulged in Eli's arms as he hefted box after box into her cottage. She really wanted to touch the smooth curve of his biceps. But it was the size of his broad chest and wide shoulders that *really* made her short of breath. "Who somehow gets under my skin!"

"To whom you feel an immediate attraction, you mean."

"He's good-looking. That's all," she said, hoping to minimize it.

"That's why you told him, out of the blue, that you have a boyfriend as if you were accusing him of hitting on you? Because he's good-looking? What were you thinking?"

"I don't know! I was merely attempting to wall off the possibility. So I wouldn't even consider it That's not *too* weird, is it?"

"You might've gotten ahead of yourself, but... I'm guessing you succeeded. I doubt he's hoping for anything now, so you can relax."

Cora took a deep breath. Jill was right. Maybe she hadn't done it gracefully, but she'd put Elijah Turner on notice that she wasn't a romantic possibility. Even if he hadn't considered her one to begin with, establishing certain boundaries was important to *her*. She needed to focus, to keep her life simple while she was here so that she could do a good job for the kids at the ranch while getting to know Aiyana. If she decided she wanted to be part of Aiyana's life, she'd eventually have to determine if Aiyana wanted to be part of hers—and break the news. Imagine how awkward it would be if the answer to that question was no and yet she was seeing Eli!

"It's better that we covered it early."

"If you say so. How's the cottage?"

"Small but cute." She wandered over to a Mason jar filled with wildflowers that someone had left on her table. It was a thoughtful touch, one she hoped Eli wasn't responsible for...

"I can't wait to see it." Jill suddenly lowered her voice. "I've got to go. My boss is here."

Cora wasn't even sure she said goodbye when they disconnected. Her attention had switched entirely to a small card she found beside the flowers.

Welcome to New Horizons. We are so excited to have you here.

Aiyana

Bending slightly, Cora put her nose to one of the delicate yellow poppies that made up the bulk of the arrangement. "I hope you'll be just as glad once you learn who I am," she said as she exhaled.

Chapter Four

"So *you're* the new art teacher."

Cora smiled at the middle-aged man with thick glasses who sat on her right side. "Yes."

"Ah. Makes sense at last."

"What makes sense?" she asked, but he didn't get the chance to answer—or even introduce himself. Aiyana stood near the circulation desk and called the staff to order. Cora felt she knew where the man had been going with that comment, anyway. Everyone thought she'd gotten the job based on her looks. Otherwise, Gary Something-or-Other would've gotten it.

"Thank you all for coming," Aiyana said. "Although we had a few of you here during the summer, handling one program or another, classes were limited. So I hope, now that the rest of you are back, you feel refreshed, because I'm anticipating one of the best years in ranch history."

As Aiyana spoke, Cora glanced around. There were thirtysomething people in the room, an assortment of teachers and support staff, but she couldn't see anyone even close to her own age. Half the people seemed to be in their forties, the other half in their fifties. A few looked even older.

She was beginning to believe Jill and her mother were right: the next year was going to be terribly lonely...

"Before we get started, let's go over a few of the changes that have occurred in the past two and a half months. First, we will have 256 students when we start classes on the twenty-eighth, up from 223 last year. That's a significant increase, so we'll have to watch out for the newcomers and help them feel at home. We also have a new football coach—Larry Sanders, who played in the pros thirteen years ago. Larry couldn't be here tonight due to a family commitment, but he's been practicing with the boys for over a month. I believe he'll be a real asset to our sports program—at least that's what Elijah tells me. As most of you know, Elijah is our athletic director in addition to many other things—basically whatever he needs to be in order for the ranch to operate smoothly."

Cora's neighbor leaned over. "Someone with real experience, huh? Maybe we'll finally win a game," he muttered.

Cora didn't respond; she was too interested in witnessing the pride on Aiyana's face when she looked at her adopted son. They were close. That was obvious without either one of them having to say a word—but as nice as that was for Elijah, Cora found it a bit disheartening. Was there any room in Aiyana's heart for her?

Cora didn't get the impression there was, but she didn't have the chance to think about it for too long. Aiyana was moving on.

"Not only do we have a new football coach, we have a new art instructor." She stretched out her hand in invitation. "Cora, will you please stand?"

Elijah's eyes seemed to cut right through Cora as she got to her feet. Why she could feel the weight of his gaze and not anyone else's, she couldn't say, but she'd been struggling to ignore him since she walked into this meeting.

After a nod to acknowledge all the smiling faces that were turned to see the new art instructor, she sank back into her seat.

Aiyana was talking about how they were going to allow student government to run the assemblies from now on when the man next to her leaned over again. "Where have you taught before?" he asked.

After his earlier comment, Cora almost provided the name of the high school that had offered her a permanent position a few weeks ago, but a quick word with Aiyana or Elijah would too easily reveal the truth, since she'd been honest with them. "I've never had a permanent position."

"You're a *brand-new* teacher?"

"Relatively new," she admitted. "I've been subbing for six years."

"Do you have any idea how difficult some of the boys who come here can be?"

Aiyana hadn't given the bad behavior Cora was likely to encounter much emphasis. But Cora had known from the beginning that this school wasn't for the well-adjusted. "I understand that most of the boys come from a very difficult background," she replied. "But it shouldn't be *too* much of a change. You should see how some regular students treat substitutes," she joked.

The man laughed but quickly sobered. "Subbing isn't easy. Kids will get away with whatever they can. Still, for an attractive young woman of your age—"

"I'm nearly thirty," she broke in, but she had to wonder—in her hurry to get close to Aiyana, had she given what she might face here enough weight?

"Still," the man said. "It won't be easy. I hope you haven't gotten in over your head."

When Cora glanced up, she happened to catch Elijah watching her. He didn't look away, as she expected him to; he continued to measure her with those enigmatic eyes. Was he experiencing any doubts about having hired her?

Possibly. *Probably.* She hated to even consider that. But if she had to fight to find her place in the world, she'd do it. She supposed, in that respect, she wasn't much different from Elijah or the other boys who'd come through here, or were still attending.

"I'll be fine," she said—and hoped it was true.

* * *

"I see you met Sean Travers."

Cora recognized Elijah's voice even before she turned to see him standing at her elbow. Why he'd put her through the discomfort approaching her was bound to cause, however, she couldn't say.

"The guy who was sitting next to me?" she asked.

"Yes. Our science teacher—or ranch pessimist, depending on how well you know him."

She nibbled at the cookie she'd just snagged from the refreshment table. "He doesn't think I'm capable of teaching here. I guess I look too young and delicate to handle the boys who act out."

"Does that shake your confidence?"

"I admit I'm a little worried. Everyone seems to believe the job should've gone to a man named Gary…"

"Seton," he filled in as he handed her a cup of punch. "Because he's local—they know him."

"But…"

"It wasn't their decision," he said simply.

She couldn't help envying him his long, dark eyelashes. She knew she had pretty eyes—guys told her that all the time—but she felt his were prettier. "No. It was yours. So…can you tell me why?"

"Why I chose you?"

"I know it isn't what they all seem to think. You made that clear earlier."

He took a sip of his own punch. "As far as I'm concerned, your competition has no…vision."

"Am I supposed to understand what that means?"

His massive shoulders lifted in a shrug. "I wasn't impressed with his work."

"You were impressed with *mine*?"

"You're talented," he said evenly. "Perhaps more than you know."

"I'm *teaching* art, not selling it. I'm guessing he was at least proficient."

Elijah finally shifted that unnerving gaze away from her. "You have to understand certain concepts to be able to teach them."

"What concepts are you specifically referring to?" she asked, but someone else approached him at that moment, interrupting, and he turned away without answering.

Since Eli fell deep into conversation with a woman who looked sixty or so and was concerned about a particular student Cora had no way of knowing, she felt awkward standing there waiting for the chance to speak to him again. So she gave them some privacy by carrying her punch over to the corner. She was looking for an unobtrusive vantage point from which to observe her birth mother. Aiyana was mingling with the staff. But then Cora saw the science teacher who'd sat next to her approach Aiyana and knew, when they both glanced in her direction, that they were talking about her. Sean Travers was expressing his reservations.

Disgruntled that this man she'd barely met would jump to conclusions based on her age and gender, and start to advocate against her, Cora finished her punch, dropped the paper cup in the wastebasket and left the library. Her phone kept vibrating in her pocket anyway, making her feel as if someone really needed to reach her.

When she got outside and felt she could check, caller ID indicated it was her father.

Gazing up at more stars than she'd ever seen in the sky before, she wandered around the campus as she spoke to him. Most of the students were away, at home if they had a home to go to, for a quick holiday before classes started in earnest, so the campus was quiet, especially this far from the outdoor basketball courts and the dorms.

"So are you going to like it there?" her father asked.

She tried to let the energy in his voice help lift the depression that had set in. "It's definitely going to be a change."

"A positive one, though, right?"

"Sure," she said, kicking a small pebble across the sidewalk.

"Whoa. Is something wrong?"

"It's just different, that's all. I'm not used to smelling manure at night. Or seeing stars that shine so bright."

"The manure can't be pleasant, but the stars sound nice."

"They are nice. And the manure isn't all that bad, not if I stay away from the livestock pens. I guess it's more that… I'm beginning to wonder what made me think I could handle teenage boys who have significant behavioral issues." She'd mostly been thinking of her own emotional issues, not the responsibility she would feel to be a guiding light to teenage boys who'd lost their way. Was she bound to disappoint Aiyana and Elijah and let her students down?

She couldn't abide the thought of failure.

"Don't make it too complicated, babe," her father said.

"In what way?"

"Everyone responds to love."

"I have to do more than love them, Dad. I have to *teach* them. And what if they won't let me?"

"If you love them, they'll trust you. Love and trust come first. Then you'll be able to teach. I promise you."

She thought of Gary Seton. Maybe he had no "vision," whatever Elijah meant by that. But she was willing to bet he'd be firmer when it came to meting out discipline. *She* didn't want to punish anyone. "I'm not sure why these people hired me," she grumbled.

"They must've seen what your mother and I see in you."

"And that is…"

"You can do anything."

Tears filled her eyes. She was tired, which made her

emotional. But she was also experiencing a little culture shock, and she missed her family already. "Maybe I was a bit hasty making the decision to come here, Dad."

"It's only for a year, honey. Do your best. That's all anyone can ask. And come see us when you can."

She wiped her cheeks as she told him she loved him. But she felt even worse after she disconnected. She had good parents. The conversation she'd just had with her father proved it yet again. So why was she betraying them?

The moment she got back to her cottage, Cora went straight to bed. She had a lot of unpacking yet to do, but she figured that could wait. She needed sleep, knew it would help her cope with all the recent changes—as well as the uncertainty.

Fortunately, she felt a lot better when she woke up. She spent the morning unpacking the rest of her belongings and stacking the cardboard from the boxes in her SUV so she could take it to a recycling center. Then she decided to go into town to look around, have lunch and buy a few groceries. Someone—she guessed Aiyana since Aiyana had also been responsible for the flowers—had put a few essentials, like eggs, bread and milk, in her fridge, but the cupboards needed to be stocked.

Cora was halfway to town when she saw a man on horseback galloping down a dirt road off to her right. She would've thought nothing of it—she could only see the rider from the back as he wove in and out of the trees between them—but she recognized the man. It was Elijah Turner!

She pulled over and angled her head to see through the passenger window, trying to get a better look. He was something else. A puzzle. What drove him? What did he want out of life? Had he put the past behind him? How did she feel about the boys who came to the ranch? Did he see himself in each one? Where were the people who'd abused him? Did he have any contact with them? Was his work enough to fulfill him? Or was he seeing someone?

Maybe he was dating around...

Cora was also curious to learn how he'd gotten that scar on his face—but equally afraid to find out. What she'd read about him scared her. She didn't want to imagine him going through any more pain and suffering than what she'd been forced to imagine when she'd read that article about him. She wondered if other people had the same reaction—if they shied away from him for fear they might have to walk into that darkness.

Movement behind him caught her eye, and she realized that he wasn't alone. He had three boys with him. It looked as though he was taking some New Horizons students out for a ride...

She glanced into her backseat. She had her camera, had brought it to take some pictures of Silver Springs she could send to Jill and her family. She still planned to do that, but her fingers itched to take a few shots of him and those boys first. She'd never seen a man sit so comfortably in the saddle as Elijah. And she loved the way he kept looking back at the boys, like a mother hen checking her chicks.

This wasn't about admiring Aiyana's adopted son so much as it was about the symbolism she saw here, she told herself as she cut the engine. He represented a man who'd not only survived tremendous difficulty but risen above it. Someone who'd conquered his demons. And now he was helping others battle theirs. There was a great deal of artistic beauty in that, and she had to capture it.

She couldn't get a clear shot from the roadside, however. There were too many trees in between.

After hiking down the embankment, she wove through the forest to get close enough. Luckily for her, or she never would've caught up with them, Elijah and the boys had stopped and were laughing and talking while drinking from a canteen Eli passed around.

She fastened her heavy telephoto lens to the expensive camera her parents had given her for Christmas last year and clicked away, using a fast shutter speed so that the pictures wouldn't turn out blurry. In one picture, she captured Elijah laughing. She'd never seen him smile, not so easily. He was in his element out here, and he cared about the boys he was with. Those two things were readily apparent; she could see it in both his body language and his expression.

Cora was disappointed when he put the lid on the canteen, slung it over his body, where he'd been carrying it before, and charged up the next hill, making it impossible for her to get any more pictures of him.

As the boys whooped and hollered in their efforts to keep up with him, she hiked back to her car. They were having a blast. She could easily imagine any problem they had disappearing while they were out enjoying the beautiful scenery and the equally beautiful weather.

Witnessing the impact Elijah was having on the students at the ranch—by taking enough interest to guide them on a ride even during their "off" period—inspired her. He was embracing the spirit of his job. Like Aiyana, he was doing it for the right reasons. And so could she. She had a lot of love to give. Who needed it more than abused, neglected and angry teens?

How are you doing today?

Her father's text came in just before Cora started her car. Better, she wrote.

Because...

Because coming here was no longer only about her. I feel like I could make a real difference with this job.

That's the spirit!

Cora responded by sending a smiley face, put her phone down and headed into town, where she took quite a few pictures. It was a great way to investigate her new surroundings. Those were the ones she posted on Instagram and sent to family and friends who were eager to see where she'd moved. But it was the photographs of Elijah and the three boys that she downloaded onto her computer when she returned that night. She spent over an hour experimenting with different filters and other bells and whistles on Photoshop. In her favorite photograph, one where Elijah was smiling at the boy to his left, the lighting was perfect as it came through the branches of the trees.

She could win a contest with that shot…

"Hail to the conquering hero," she muttered before she set her computer aside and turned off the light so that she could get some sleep.

Chapter Five

Over the next few days, Cora put her classroom in order by making sure the large, commercial-sized kiln and sixteen throwing wheels in the pottery room were clean and in good repair. She also took stock of the clay and other supplies. The teacher before her had done a respectable job caring for the equipment and maintaining the necessary inventory, so it wasn't too overwhelming of a job. She obtained permission to order some glazes she'd been hoping to get, as well as a new set of colored pencils and paintbrushes for each student, so she'd at least have the supplies needed to start the year off right.

By the end of the week, Cora was feeling pretty encouraged about beginning school on Monday. She'd been running into more and more students as the boys returned to the ranch and was looking forward to meeting the rest. Other than texting and calling her old friends and her brother, who promised to come out and see her soon, she'd had virtually no social life since she arrived, so she figured more distraction, work and activity would help fill that gap. The neighbor opposite to Sean Travers, Doug Maggleby, a math teacher at the school, chatted with her whenever he caught her out and about. But she'd started to avoid him, where possible. The more he talked, the more uncomfortable he made her. He liked to rave about politics, and she rarely agreed with his opinion. He'd also mentioned taking her to the movies even though he was clearly too old for her. She wasn't looking forward to having to say no, but knew that was coming. So instead of visiting with him in the evenings like she had the first few nights, she'd sneak out of her bungalow and walk down to the pond to watch the sunset or stop by the horses' pen to say good-night. If Mr. Maggleby happened to be in his yard working in his fall garden, however, she'd settle for having a glass of wine in her cottage and reading a book or going over her lesson plans.

She'd seen very little of Elijah since taking those photographs of him horseback riding with the boys. Although she wasn't pleased by the fact, she'd developed a habit of looking for him whenever she was out. Occasionally, she'd spot him at a distance and couldn't help admiring what she saw. But he seemed extra busy getting the ranch ready for the fall semester, so she was fairly certain she was the last thing on *his* mind.

Aiyana had been especially busy, too. Since Betty May had handled the purchase requisition for the art supplies, Cora had had no interaction with her birth mother—not until Friday afternoon. She was in the cafeteria between lunch and dinner, nibbling on a chocolate chip cookie while she finished reading the orientation materials she'd been given, when Aiyana came in, poured herself a cup of coffee and walked over to join Cora.

"Hello." Instantly self-conscious, Cora closed the manual as her "boss" sat down.

"How are you holding up, dear?" Aiyana asked.

"Good." She cleared her throat. "Great."

"I'm relieved to hear it—and glad to find you here. This time of year is so crazy for me. I apologize that I haven't had the chance to check on you. Did you get the supplies you requested?"

"Not yet. But last I heard they've been ordered, so they should arrive soon. Thanks for giving the okay on that."

She took a drink of her coffee. "I told you how I feel about art. That isn't where I choose to skimp."

"I have to admit your attitude is refreshing. I'm not used to art being much of a priority."

"The practicalities of running a school can often get in the way of even the best intentions," she said. "Fortunately, right now, we've got some wealthy benefactors who are giving us the support we need." She winked. "Makes a difference when we have a fair number of students with rich—and sometimes famous—parents."

"Are we talking movie stars?" Cora hadn't considered that possibility, but she supposed, since they weren't far from LA, it was logical.

"A few. Others are the children of producers and movie execs, attorneys, doctors, that sort of thing."

"Are the wealthy kids ones who are typically loved, or…"

Her lips curved into a rueful smile. "Oh, they're loved, just a little more generously than would probably be best. From what I've seen, being given too much can be as difficult as being given too little."

"Doesn't that create quite a disparity? I mean…you mentioned taking in orphans who have no one to support them."

"We have some of the richest *and* some of the poorest students in the state. But we make it clear from the beginning that everyone is on an equal footing here at the ranch. There is no favoritism, no bending of the rules because of who their parents are."

"I can't imagine that goes over very well—not for people who are used to receiving preferential treatment."

"I've lost several students over that policy," she admitted. "All parents agree to it when they enroll their child— but can change their minds once they want or need special treatment." She pushed a strand of loose hair out of her face. "Regardless, I won't bend. To me it's a matter of integrity. And, if a parent will stand behind me, their son usually settles down and begins to learn the lessons they were hoping we'd teach him."

Cora swallowed another bite of her cookie. "How does that play out in a social setting—for the kids, I mean?"

Aiyana took another sip of coffee. "Depends. We take a hard line on bullying, too—watch carefully for it. Most get the message early on that the rules are firmer here, but fair to all, and life falls into a sustainable rhythm. I don't think we're too terribly different from other high schools— all schools have some behavioral problems."

"But you've taken on the behavioral problems other schools can no longer cope with. Doesn't that ever make you feel...intimidated?"

"I wouldn't want to go back and start over—I can tell you that," she said with a mirthless chuckle. "But now that we're up and running, and I've got the momentum that comes from doing this for so long, it's easier than it was. Still, I couldn't continue without the community support I've received, not to mention the devoted teachers we have here—and Elijah, who has such a knack for communicating with these boys. Even if I can't get one to behave, he usually can."

Cora pictured Aiyana's son on top of that horse. "Elijah's your secret weapon."

"Absolutely."

She studied Aiyana's face. Her mother was so pretty despite the lines that were beginning to appear around her eyes and mouth and the ribbons of gray in her hair. "I hope you don't mind me asking, but..."

"Ask me anything," she said.

"I was wondering what nationality you are."

She seemed surprised by the question—that Cora would have any interest in that—but not put off. "My mother is a Nicaraguan immigrant. My father was a white farmhand in the Central Valley."

"Are they still alive?"

"They are. But my mother is no longer with my father. He was an abusive man, so I don't have any contact with him, either. For many years now she's been with the farmer who employed them both and has been so much happier. What about you? What nationality are you?"

Cora thought it might be too coincidental if she were to say she was part Nicaraguan, but that was good to know— filled in one of the many blanks in her life. Aiyana had said her father was white; from her skin tone, Cora assumed hers was, too. "I'm a mix, I think."

"And your parents? Where are they?"

"In LA. My father's a financial planner. My mother's sort of a…socialite."

She smiled at that. "Do you have siblings?"

"An older brother who's larger than life and terribly handsome. Like a lot of people in LA, he's a movie producer. What about you?"

"I have one older brother and two younger brothers, but I don't see my younger brothers very often."

She seemed noticeably saddened by that. "They don't live close?"

"My brothers are all over California. One owns a winery in Napa. One is in banking in San Francisco. The oldest runs the farm for my mom and stepdad in Los Banos, where I grew up."

"Are they all married?"

"Yes. With kids. What about your brother?"

Suppressing her curiosity about why Aiyana had never married, Cora answered the question. "Still playing the field."

"Sounds like my sons."

"Where are they all? I mean, besides Eli, of course."

"Gavin, my second oldest, has a house in town but works here. He's a handyman, can fix anything."

"Really?" Cora had been around for five days, yet she couldn't recall ever seeing a handyman. "Was he at the meeting on Monday?"

"No. He's not someone who likes to get involved in the administration aspect of the ranch. He prefers to remain in the background, which is why he lives in town."

"How old is he?"

"Twenty-eight. I adopted him three years after I adopted Elijah. Then there's Dallas. He's twenty-five and a mountain climber, so he's usually off, traveling to remote destinations all over the world. I don't get to see him much." She seemed to regret that but moved on. "Seth is twenty-three. He recently graduated from UC Berkeley, wants to be a sculptor. That's one of the reasons I love art so much," she confided. "I'm not sure what I would've done with him if I hadn't been able to reach him in that way..."

"He has...emotional issues?"

"Anger issues, mostly. I seem to gravitate to the most damaged of the boys. I can't help trying to make them whole."

Did Aiyana always accomplish that? Or were some of her sons *too* damaged? "Let's see—Elijah, Gavin, Dallas and Seth. That's four sons, but I heard you have eight," Cora said. "What about the others?"

"Ryan and Taylor are twins. Well, they're not actually *related*, but we call them twins because they're the same age and have done just about everything together since they met here at the ranch. They're still in college. Ryan wants to be a planetary scientist, and Taylor has set his sights on becoming a theoretical physicist. They're both too brilliant for their own good," she added. "Now that they're actually applying themselves."

"Where do they go to school?"

"MIT. Then I have Liam and Bentley, who go here. Liam's a senior. Bentley's a sophomore."

"I wonder if I've seen either one of them around."

"Not yet. They've been with Dallas at Yosemite the past ten days. He's teaching them how to climb."

"That's nice of him."

"They *live* to spend time with their older brothers." She lowered her voice. "He better not let them get hurt, though."

"It's a scary sport." Cora dusted the cookie crumbs off her "boyfriend" jeans. "Would you ever consider adopting more?"

Finished with her coffee, Aiyana pushed the cup aside. "I keep telling myself I need to stop. But every couple of years, it seems as if there's at least one more I'm dying to take home with me."

"That means...maybe?"

"I guess. It'll depend on the circumstances."

So she would take in another boy if she felt he needed her that much, Cora decided. "Did you always want a big family?" she asked and then held her breath. She thought this might be the most revealing question yet, that it might give her some clue as to why Aiyana hadn't wanted *her*, but Aiyana's face grew shuttered as she shook her head.

"No. Never thought I'd have any kids."

Cora was dying to ask why, but there was something so forbidding in the sudden change in Aiyana's expression and body language that she could tell it would be too intrusive. Aiyana had essentially slammed the door shut on that subject, and she didn't stick around long enough to give Cora much of a chance to talk about anything else.

"I'd better go." She reclaimed her empty cup as she stood. "It's been wonderful having a chance to chat, but I've got a lot to do before the pizza party tonight. You're coming, right?"

Cora had found a flyer taped to her door when she got back to her cottage last night announcing a Kickoff Party for all the teachers at a place called Moonstruck Pizza in town. "I haven't made up my mind, to be honest."

"Oh, don't miss it," she said. "The entire staff gets together the Friday before school starts to celebrate the end of summer and the beginning of a new year. It's a tradition."

"And the students? They stay on campus?"

"Yes. The floor monitors keep an eye on them. So come to the party. It'll give everyone a chance to get to know you. And there'll be plenty of pizza and beer—and karaoke, if you sing."

"I sing a little," Cora said, but that was an understatement. She sang a lot. She and a handful of friends liked to compete in various local contests, enjoyed standing behind a mic. And she really needed to get out and have some fun. She just hoped Doug Maggleby wouldn't be too determined to monopolize her time. She could easily imagine spending the evening trying to dodge him.

"So you'll be there?" Aiyana seemed eager for her company.

At that point, Cora didn't feel as if she could refuse— not if it might afford her a few minutes more with her birth mother. "Sure. Why not?" she said, but as soon as she agreed, she began to wonder if Elijah would be part of the festivities. Then she chided herself for having the desire to see him. She was letting herself get quite a "thing" for Aiyana's handsome son, even though she barely knew him and he'd made it clear he wasn't interested in *her.*

He *was* there. Cora spotted Elijah as soon as she walked into the pizza parlor and hated herself for suddenly being so glad she'd come. She didn't need to get her heart broken; she was trying to mend it by moving here, to finally get over the sense of rejection her adoption had engendered.

But she figured she shouldn't be *too* hard on herself.

She didn't yet know anyone other than the staff she'd been introduced to at the school, so it wasn't all that surprising she'd fixate on the one man she'd met who was in her age bracket—especially when she factored in how darned handsome he was.

She couldn't get hurt if he never responded, anyway. His disinterest made the attraction safe. So she figured she might as well enjoy the view he provided, maybe even indulge in a few harmless fantasies. If allowing him to fuel her imagination helped pass the time and made her stint in Silver Springs more enjoyable, why not?

Feeling slightly empowered by the fact that she had no expectations, she smiled widely when he looked up. Once she found a seat and everyone went back to chatting and drinking their sodas and beer, she even winked at him, since he was still watching her.

He didn't wink in return—or even smile. But he didn't look away, either. He studied her that much more closely, as if he was trying to figure out what she was up to.

Since Doug Maggleby insisted on crowding as close to her as possible, she was glad when the pizza finally arrived. Doing her best to keep interaction with him to a minimum, she focused on the female English teacher on her other side, a recent divorcée with two kids, neither of whom was with her now because her ex had picked them up for the weekend.

Cora also kept an eye on Aiyana. She hoped to speak to her mother again—at some length, if the opportunity presented itself. She now knew that she had living grandparents and uncles and where they all lived and what they did for work! It was a revelation, considering the dearth of information she'd had until six months ago. There were a lot of other things Cora wanted to know—but Aiyana was always surrounded by an eager group of teachers or other staff.

Everyone who worked for her liked her, Cora realized. They all seemed to bask in whatever attention she gave them. Thanks to that, there was no chance for Cora to approach her while they waited for the pizza, and Aiyana left shortly after it came, before the karaoke even started.

"Are you leaving, too?" Cora asked Darci Spinoza, the English teacher she'd been chatting with most of the night, when another group from their party started to say goodbye.

"No way," she replied. "You said you were going to sing. Since I don't have a voice, and wouldn't have the nerve to perform in front of a crowd even if I did, I'm waiting to hear you."

"Me, too," Doug chimed in.

Although Cora was grateful that Darci would be staying, she wished Doug would find other friends. Her other neighbor, Sean, sat in the corner with a couple of people. Why couldn't Doug go over there? He was drinking too much, which made him feel free to touch her...

Briefly, she considered going home herself, to avoid him, but she hated to miss her chance to sing. And Elijah was still there. He stood with his back against the wall and a beer in his hand, talking to a man she'd never met. Because that man was somewhere close to their age, was part of the group from the school and seemed so comfortable around Elijah, she guessed it was Gavin, the handyman Aiyana had mentioned and Elijah's younger brother. Tall and thin, he had a beard and several tattoos on his arms. He was handsome, but not nearly as handsome as Elijah.

Once the karaoke started, Cora tried to ignore the bothersome, overbearing and balding Doug and went to the mic to sing "Jolene." On subsequent trips she performed "I Hope You Dance" and "Wrecking Ball." After that, Darci, Doug and several others kept prodding her to get up again. Some people even made requests—and a table of four men, who hadn't been part of their group but had come in later, started sending her drinks.

"Those guys are really into you," Doug said. "But of course they would be. Who wouldn't like a gorgeous woman like you?"

Cora couldn't help leaning away from his sour breath. He was getting so close when he talked it felt as if he was trying to look down her blouse.

Catching her recoil, Darci gave her a nudge. "I think it's time for Doug to go to bed, but…he can't drive in that condition."

No, he couldn't. Someone had to see that he got home safely, and Cora was the obvious choice. They lived right next door to each other, after all—and Sean had already left. "Is there any way we could call him a taxi or even an Uber?" she whispered back.

Darci laughed at the question. "Not in this small of a town. There's no such thing here. But if you'd rather not take him, I will."

Cora couldn't ask her new friend to go twenty minutes out of the way. Darci had already told her that she lived in town. "No, I'll do it. Just…help me get him to my car, okay?"

"Sure, I can do that."

They had no trouble persuading Doug that he shouldn't drive, not once he learned he'd be riding with her—and that she'd bring him back to get his car in the morning. At that point, Cora forgot about Elijah. She was too intent on stopping Doug from copping a feel as she and Darci helped him outside. She'd just unlocked her car so they could put him in the passenger seat when Elijah came out of the pizza parlor along with the man she'd guessed was Gavin.

Darci said good-night to them, so Cora looked up and said the same. She expected the brothers to go on their way, possibly to a bar if they weren't ready to go home for the night, but "Gavin" waited on the curb while Elijah came around to where they were trying to get Doug in the car.

"Here, I'll take him." Slipping Doug's arm around his neck, Eli started to cart the math teacher off.

Cora was so relieved she almost couldn't hide it. "Are you sure?"

"Why would I go home with you when I could go home with *her*?" Doug protested, his voice overloud and his expression bordering on belligerent.

"Because I'm not giving you any choice," Elijah said, and that was the end of it. Cora was fairly certain Doug knew better than to balk, that he'd be stupid to try to stand up to Elijah, because he didn't object again. "Gavin" met his brother and took hold of Doug's other arm, and Cora was left to drive home alone.

"That was nice," she said on a long exhale.

Darci smiled as if she was holding something back. "What?" Cora asked.

"Eli could tell you weren't comfortable, that you didn't want to take Doug home."

She straightened. Of course she didn't want her drunk octopus of a neighbor in the car with her. But Darci was intimating something more than that. "What do you mean? Elijah was clear across the room. How would he know anything?"

"You're kidding, right? He's been watching you all night. Every time I glanced up, he had his eyes on you. I've known him for a year and have never seen him so focused on a woman. I think Doug got a little too close to what Eli wants himself."

"That's not true," Cora argued. "Eli was simply being a stand-up guy by putting me out of my misery—knew he was better equipped to handle Doug in his current condition than I am."

"If you say so." Her singsong voice indicated she didn't

believe that at all, but she didn't belabor the point. "It was great spending time with you," she said. "I'm glad you've come to town. What with the divorce and dealing with my ex since I moved here, it's been hard to make friends. And now it's too late to be that new girl who gets introduced around. So…I'm happy to meet someone who's starting fresh and might be open to getting to know me."

"I'm definitely open to that," Cora said.

"Even though I'm quite a bit older than you?"

Cora waved her words away. "Age doesn't matter when it comes to friendship."

"That takes care of that, then. Now maybe I'll have someone to do something with when the weekends roll around and my kids are with their dad."

"I'm sure I'll be looking for a chance to get off the campus." She waved as Darci walked down the street to her car, but her mind wasn't on her new friend. She kept mulling over what Darci had said about Elijah, and realized she was right. Elijah wasn't just being a good guy in general when he took Doug off her hands. He was looking out for her—*specifically*.

Chapter Six

Elijah found Cora leaning up against the side of his truck when he came out of Doug Maggleby's house.

"Thanks for putting my neighbor to bed for me," she said as he walked toward her. "I was not looking forward to that."

He could tell. She didn't like Doug touching her, and he hadn't liked it much, either. "No need to thank me. He's not your responsibility."

"He's not yours, either."

He shrugged. "It's not like I was going out of my way."

She tucked her long brown hair behind her ears. "So you didn't do it for me?"

He *had* done it for her, but he preferred to downplay that part. "No."

He assumed she'd let it go at that, but she gave him a skeptical once-over.

"What?" he said.

"You're so full of it."

He felt his eyebrows go up. He wasn't sure he'd ever had another woman say something like that to him before. "Excuse me?"

"You're acting like you're not interested in me, but…"

This new girl was nothing if not unpredictable, Elijah decided. She didn't play by the usual rules—at least not the old-fashioned rules he'd grown accustomed to living out here in the country. Problem was…she was right. He *was* interested in her. But he couldn't let himself act on that interest. "What makes you think so?" He rested both hands on the truck, one on either side of her. He figured if she was going to challenge him, he was going to challenge her right back.

But she didn't flounder for a response, didn't back down. She wasn't intimidated in the least, even though he had her penned between his arms and virtually towered over her.

Her gaze lowered to his mouth. "The way you look at me."

He tensed with the desire to press her up against his truck and kiss her soundly. She was baiting him, trying to see what he would do, which left him torn. Part of him felt she deserved to get a bit more than she bargained for. The other part knew better than to let things move in that direction. He'd been keeping his distance from her for a reason.

"*You're* the one who said you had a boyfriend," he said. "Maybe you've forgotten the other day. I was carrying in your boxes, you were acting all concerned, as if that might mean you owed me something, and then you said—"

"I remember," she broke in.

"So…what's up with that? Where'd your boyfriend go?"

She lifted her chin defiantly. "I broke up with him over a month ago."

"You lied?"

Still, she didn't back down. "Basically."

"Because…"

For the first time her confidence seemed to waver. "I don't know. It doesn't make sense. I… I felt something I didn't want to feel. And I panicked."

He was so astounded by her honesty he wasn't sure how to respond. So he went with the obvious—what he'd been using to warn himself off since she'd arrived in Silver Springs. "I'm your boss, Cora."

"*That's* what's holding you back? Professional integrity?"

"One of the things, yes. This school—the boys here—are important to me."

"One doesn't necessarily cancel out the other."

"I hired you because I thought you'd be the best teacher for the job." He'd also thought he'd be able to ignore how alive he felt whenever he was around her, but he'd never expected her to confront him so directly. That forced the issue out in the open, made the attraction more difficult to ignore. "I'm sure my mother wouldn't thank me for giving her new art instructor reason to quit and leave."

That brief moment of insecurity he'd noted before seemed to fall by the wayside. "You're sure dating me would go in that direction?"

His ex-girlfriend said he walled himself off, refused to give anything emotionally. And she probably had the right of it. The shrink Aiyana used to send him to said a lot of the same stuff. Dr. Anderson told him he needed to learn how to open up, which sounded good in theory but he couldn't figure out how. He'd finally refused to continue therapy. He wanted to close the door on his past and make sure it was never opened again, not rehash those painful memories.

"It's not like I've never been down this road," he said. "I've been in a number of relationships. Enough to know my limitations."

"*All* those relationships ended badly?"

He'd been taught to believe he was so terrible, so *unacceptable*, that he'd been painfully shy around girls growing up. He hadn't even started dating until he was twenty, and he'd only had three fairly serious—and fairly short—relationships since. "Let's just say…I don't have a high success ratio when it comes to women."

"You and Aiyana are *very* close."

"That's different."

"Love is love. You had to decide to trust her at some point."

"Not everyone has her patience," he said. "She was so determined to love me, I had no choice."

"And those other women?"

The scent of her perfume rose to his nostrils. He liked the way she smelled, wanted to touch all that soft-looking skin. The temptation to slide his hand up her shirt burned through him like hard liquor. "As I said, it's not the same thing."

"Because it involves physical intimacy? What, exactly, are your 'limitations'? Are you saying you can't have sex?"

He was pretty sure she was goading him. At least, he hoped she was, that she didn't really believe he was incapable. Either way, he was eager to put the question to rest. "My body works fine. It's my inability to make you feel loved and 'validated.' I think that was the word."

"So I'd only get hurt if I got involved with you."

"Yes. You'd essentially be getting a locked box."

He was being transparent, completely up front. She was the one who'd set that tone. So it surprised him when she barked out a laugh. "You think you're doing me a favor by staying away!"

He was trying to adhere to the decisions he'd made after that last ugly blowout with Tina. He'd been glad for the peace and balance he'd found since they broke up a year ago. But twelve months was a long time to go without a woman... "Essentially."

"Well, you're taking a lot for granted, Mr. Turner. First of all, how do you know I'm going to want you to love me?"

"Experience," he said wryly. "I have yet to encounter the opposite problem."

"You're in such high demand that you've grown arrogant?"

"Failure hardly makes me arrogant. It does, however, make me want to avoid running into the same brick wall."

"I see. Well, you don't have to look out for me. I'm a big girl."

"Which, of course, you'll say until our relationship doesn't progress. Then you'll quit your job and go back to LA."

She rolled her eyes. "I'm only here for one year. No matter what happens, I'm not going to quit my job."

Was she as resilient as she pretended? He couldn't help getting his hopes up. He was already starting to imagine her on her back, her hair falling across his pillow... "Then you have a decision to make."

"What kind of decision?"

"Are you up for a strictly physical relationship? Because if that's all you're after, I'd be happy to accommodate you. I have no doubt I could satisfy you there."

She studied him. "That's all *you're* interested in?"

"Yes. I'm sorry." He wasn't about to go down the same road he'd been down before. But he wasn't sure why he was apologizing, since she sounded almost...relieved by this news.

"You're *sure*? *I* could never hurt *you*?"

"No. I'm too good at keeping my gloves up." He'd been trained from a young age...

She nodded slowly. "Okay. I'll think about it."

That didn't sound as though she'd make up her mind as quickly as he was hoping. "Any chance you could think fast?"

He wanted to kiss her so badly; the way she chewed on her bottom lip made him sort of light-headed. "We should probably give it a few weeks. See how we feel," she replied.

"*Weeks?* Does it have to take that long? Because I've already made up my mind."

She seemed uncertain. "There is something I should probably tell you..."

"And that is..."

More lip nibbling. "I've never had a strictly physical relationship."

He shifted his gaze from her lips to her eyes. "Not even a one-night stand?"

"No."

"*What?* You're from LA!"

Her expression changed to one of outrage—until she realized he was joking. "Don't even start with those stereotypes," she grumbled. "Or I'll go for the country bumpkin stuff."

Somehow, he'd underestimated her. She wasn't making it easy for him to ignore the attraction he felt. He liked her spunk. "Can you at least tell me what my chances are?" he asked, leaning a little closer.

"*I'm* the one who approached *you*, so…I'd say they're pretty decent."

"What made you approach me?" he asked, because that was a game changer. Otherwise, he would've continued to skirt around her indefinitely.

"There's just something about you."

All the things he could say to coax her, to convince her she wouldn't regret spending the night with him rose to his lips. But he knew it wouldn't be fair to put any pressure on her. She could *easily* regret the arrangement he proposed. And he didn't want that.

Taking her hand, he held it to his chest so that she could feel how hard his heart was beating. Maybe he couldn't promise her forever, but she wanted him. She'd just said so. And he wanted her.

Her hand moved slowly over his pectoral muscles in a curious caress that made him hard as a rock. He almost kissed her, was tempted to use his body to convince her if he couldn't allow himself to use his voice. But as soon as he dipped his head, she seemed to understand they were only seconds away from "too late." Once they crossed that line there would be no going back. One spark could cause them both to go up in flames.

"Like I said, I'll think about it." Pulling away, she started up the drive.

Disappointment bit deep. He stood there without reacting for several seconds, trying to overcome the letdown. Then he said, "Wait."

She didn't come back to him, but she turned, so he walked over and held out his hand. "Where's your phone?"

When she pulled it from her pocket and handed it to him, he put in his number and gave it back to her. "In case the answer is yes. Maybe it won't take as long as you think."

Cora stared at Elijah's number for at least an hour after he left. She switched between the contact information he'd put in her phone and the picture she'd taken of him out on that ride. She loved that picture so much. And yet…they'd never really spent any time together. It was ridiculous that she'd feel so compelled to call him.

She was just lonely, she told herself. She'd made a big change, was out of her element. She needed to forget about him and concentrate on what she'd come here to do, which was to teach and get to know Aiyana. She was part Nicaraguan. She had grandparents. She had uncles. These were the things she'd hoped to seek out. Her plans didn't include Elijah.

But she couldn't have anything serious with Elijah, anyway. Not without telling him that she was Aiyana's biological daughter. And she wasn't ready to do that. So he'd offered her the perfect solution: the chance to fulfill the desire he evoked without expectation.

After another ten minutes spent pacing around her small cottage, she decided to walk over to the pond. She thought sitting on the dock with the moon shining down on the water might help calm her mind. But even there, she was restless—too restless to remain on the jetty. Eventually, she made her way over to the horses' pen where she hoped, with the animals, she wouldn't feel quite so alone.

"There you are, big boy," she crooned, petting the nose of Elijah's giant horse when it ambled over to see her. "Looks like you're not getting much sleep tonight, either."

"You okay?"

Startled by the sound of Elijah's voice, Cora turned to see a dark figure sitting on the fence of the llama pen not far away, in the shadow of the nearby barn.

She pressed a hand to her chest to compensate for the shock he'd given her. "How long have you been there?"

"Since before you came out."

"You saw me, and you didn't say anything?"

"I was considering it."

"It took you a while to decide!"

"I wasn't sure you wanted to be disturbed."

Somehow it seemed like fate that they would run into each other again tonight. Or maybe she'd been subconsciously hoping for that, hoping for another opportunity, without actually having to call him. Although she'd never seen his house, she knew he lived on this part of the ranch, near the animals. She was hesitant to admit it, but, deep down, she was fairly certain that was why she'd come over here so often already. She'd been hoping to see him all along. "What are *you* doing out here?" she asked.

"Same thing you are, I suppose."

"You can't sleep."

"I have something on my mind."

"And that is…"

"You."

Cora squinted across the distance between them, trying to make out his expression. He was lonely, too, she realized. As much as he tried to pretend otherwise, he had to be. He was so aloof, so careful to warn most everyone away. She was no psychologist, but after what he'd been through, that had to be a defense mechanism. And what he'd said about Aiyana seemed to prove it. By his own admission, Aiyana had only busted through his reserve because she wouldn't take no for an answer.

Maybe that was what getting close to him required— the ability to love without expectation, without measuring or demanding anything in return. Cora could understand why that might be the case. He was tired of disappointing the women he dated, tired of feeling inadequate when they became disappointed. She'd sensed that in what he'd had to say earlier. There'd been a degree of fatalism, as if he'd given up.

His previous girlfriends had probably wanted to establish a regular relationship, one that escalated toward marriage. So they had an agenda, of sorts. Cora, on the other hand, had no agenda. She wasn't looking for a long-term relationship, couldn't have one with him, anyway, not without a very honest conversation she wasn't willing to have.

So…what if she just gave him someone to be with while she was here, some meaningful intimacy that was warm and supportive without pushing him for anything more?

"Sounds like you could use a massage," she said.

There was a moment of silence. Then he said, "Are you offering to give me one?"

She could tell he wasn't really asking about a massage, just as she knew he understood her answer wouldn't be strictly limited to one. "Sure."

"Tonight—or do I have to wait a few weeks?"

She chuckled. "Don't push your luck."

The darkness made it difficult to tell for sure, but she was fairly certain she'd gotten a smile out of him.

"You wouldn't be out here if you weren't as taken with the idea as I am," he said.

"You have a point, I suppose."

"You're not going to pretend otherwise?"

"No. Should we go to your place—or mine?"

He hopped off the fence and came toward her. "Mine."

"Any particular reason?"

"I don't have neighbors."

"Mr. Maggleby does tend to keep tabs on me."

"Mr. Maggleby is probably down for the count, but my house would still be better."

Cora drew a steadying breath as he advanced. She'd be spending the night with him. She'd just made the commitment, wouldn't feel good about backing out now.

Fortunately, she didn't want to. But her motives weren't *entirely* altruistic. She'd been craving the opportunity to touch him since the first day she'd met him.

And now she was going to have her chance.

Chapter Seven

Elijah's small A-frame was the most isolated house on the ranch and the hardest to reach, which suited him well, Cora thought as he showed her inside and closed the door behind them. He had plenty of privacy here. She got the impression that few people were ever invited inside, and that included the students he cared so much about. This was his place of retreat where he could put some distance between him and other people, since people were what he probably considered to be the biggest challenge life had to offer. Everything else seemed to come easy for him.

"Would you like a drink?" he asked.

Cora shook her head. "No. I'm good."

"Are you sure? Maybe a glass of wine?" Now that he had her inside, he was treating her as if she might bolt if he wasn't careful or courteous enough. That was another thing that made her wonder if he wasn't quite comfortable with having company. She got the impression he almost didn't know what to do with her—how to get from where they were in this moment to where he hoped to go, which wasn't in keeping with how he behaved in every other circumstance she'd noted so far.

"Okay." She relented, thinking that might help. "I'll have a glass of wine."

While he opened a bottle and poured, she wandered around his living room, which was very utilitarian—so utilitarian that the walls were completely bare. She couldn't find one thing that defined him as a person, nothing that spoke of who he was or what he liked, even on the shelves or counters. She'd never seen a house stripped down to the bare essentials before. The men she'd known had a tendency to decorate sparsely, but still.

Was it just that Elijah didn't know how to make a house a home? Or was the ability to reveal even that much of himself also locked inside the "box" he'd mentioned?

"Aren't *you* going to have one?" she asked when he handed her a glass and stood back to watch her drink it.

"No."

So much for letting a drink ease them into the evening… "Why not?"

"I'm not interested."

He was too single-minded to drink right now, Cora decided. He knew what he wanted, and it wasn't wine. But he was trying to wait his turn. "So you were merely being polite by offering me one."

"I thought you might enjoy it."

He seemed to feel as if he needed to take certain steps for her sake, as if he'd memorized a set of "rules" for how to be successful in such situations—and that included putting whatever *she* wanted first.

Setting her glass aside, she stepped up to him. She could tell he was dying to touch her, saw his hands curl into fists and his muscles tense as he wrestled with his self-control. For some reason, he was trying to let her make the first move. She supposed he wanted some reassurance that she wasn't going to suddenly change her mind. Or maybe he merely wanted to be confident he wasn't pressuring her into anything. Regardless, he was far more wary now that they were alone and behind closed doors than he'd been at his truck earlier. But they'd never had any real chance of getting intimate there, so maybe that was why.

What'd happened to him in the past had influenced *everything*, even the way he approached sex, she realized. He didn't trust other people, didn't trust *her*. "How long has it been for you?" she asked.

"Since…"

"Since you've been with a woman."

"A year."

No wonder he watched her like a wolf chasing a rabbit. That was a long time to go without for a man his age—at least it would be a long time to the men she knew in LA. But Eli lived in a small town and had the reputation of the ranch to consider—and she knew the pain that hid behind that handsome face. As normal as he came off, every once in a while there was something in his eyes that reminded her of an animal that'd been beaten so often it growled or showed its teeth even when someone tried to be kind. He craved what she was offering, couldn't bring himself to skirt around her and continue on his way, as he most likely preferred. So he was waiting for the perfect moment— when he could safely snatch it away. Were he anyone else, she felt certain he would've reached for her already…

"These encounters don't come with a script," she said.

"Meaning…"

"You don't have to serve me wine, or…or check anything else off a list."

"I'm merely trying to make sure you get what you need. I may be sort of…limited in what I can offer you, but I'm not a *completely* selfish bastard. If you'll tell me what you want, what you like, I'll give it to you."

"I don't have a punch list, Eli. That's what I'm saying. But I'm pretty sure we can figure out what we *both* like." His nostrils flared when she lifted his hand to her breast. "Does this help?"

Elijah wished it was easier to go without human touch. His life would be so much simpler. But nothing else felt like a woman. He tried to hold himself in check, to remain in control. He didn't want to overwhelm or frighten Cora, had been trying to be measured and kind. But once she put her mouth on his, and he could feel the weight of her breast in his palm, something snapped. She didn't have to do anything more. He started kissing her so hungrily that he could hardly catch his breath. And, within moments, he was peeling off her clothes, so anxious to get to bare skin that it felt like he couldn't wait another second.

He thought she might be put off. On some level, he knew he was being pretty aggressive, probably *overly* aggressive. But she had her hands in his hair and clung to him as if she was just as caught up in him as he was her. So if she was put off, he couldn't tell.

He hoped it wasn't something he'd learn about in the morning. To prevent that, he promised himself he'd take their lovemaking slower as he carried her down the hall to his bedroom.

Once there, he made an honest effort to do just that, but her kisses were so hot and wet, and she was sucking on his neck and licking his nipples. She was even biting him, just not so hard that it hurt.

Although his shirt was already on the floor, he still had his jeans on as they rolled around in his bed. Since everything he touched felt so damn good, he forgot about taking it slow and gentle. If anything, he felt the compulsion to make everything go harder and faster.

Fortunately, she seemed to be perfectly happy. With a promising smile, she unzipped his pants.

He gasped as her fingers closed around him and, only moments later, he was naked, too.

To his credit, he took a moment to admire her full breasts, small waist and the appealing flare of her hips. She had no hair *anywhere*, which, coming from LA certainly didn't surprise him, but he'd never seen a woman so bare. He liked the way she looked lying beneath him in the moonlight streaming through his window. She was as beautiful and soft as he'd expected.

Dimly, he thought about all the things he could do to bring her to climax. He planned to do every single one before he took his own pleasure. He wanted to make sure she was glad she'd agreed to be with him tonight. But once he began to suckle her breasts, she arched into him as if she craved him inside her.

"Okay. Hang on. Let me…let me take care of you first," he said.

"I'm ready," she gasped when he slid his hand between her legs.

He groaned as he encountered the slickness he was hoping to find. She *felt* ready. But burying himself inside her, this soon, wouldn't be slowing down.

"Do you have a condom?" she asked.

Fortunately, he did—in the nightstand. But he barely managed to roll it on before she pulled him on top of her and wrapped her legs around his hips—an unmistakable invitation and one he couldn't refuse.

He felt shaky as he pushed inside her. She was so wet, so tight he had to hold himself still. Otherwise, he wouldn't have even half a chance of making her come. He didn't want to be the only one who was fulfilled tonight. Then he wouldn't have done *anything* right.

"God, you feel good," he murmured, running his mouth up her neck.

"So do you," she said. "I guess it's true what they say about guys with big hands and big feet."

That comment took him so much by surprise that he almost laughed, but she didn't give him time. She grabbed hold of him—to pull him deeper inside her—and encouraged him to thrust.

"Give me a minute." He could hardly recognize his own voice it sounded so hoarse. "You're going to be disappointed if you don't."

Crooking her arm around his neck to bring him closer,

she pulled his bottom lip into her mouth. "Quit *thinking*," she whispered.

He shook his head. "You don't understand. It's been a long time for me. I'm not going to make it."

"So what? Let go. Do it any way you want." Her breath, hot in his ear, was followed by her tongue.

Her words, the freedom she gave him, sent a fresh deluge of testosterone through him, which did nothing to help his control. But if she wasn't going to help him hold out, he figured he was facing a losing battle. So he closed his eyes and drove into her with an abandon he'd rarely allowed himself before, and felt the pleasure of each thrust escalate to the point that his whole body shuddered when he hit climax.

"Goose bumps," she said as she ran a hand down his arm. "That must've been a nice one."

He stared down at her while trying to catch his breath. "It was. But I know it was too fast for you. I'm sorry."

"I enjoyed watching you," she said. "I think you needed to let loose."

Suddenly, he was *so* tired. "Give me an hour or so, and I'll redeem myself. I promise," he said as he curled around her. But he fell into such a deep sleep that it was morning when he woke up, and by then she was gone.

Elijah had a hard time being selfish. That was the most significant fact Cora had learned about him while she was in his bed. As she drove to town the following morning to meet Darci for breakfast, she couldn't help chuckling as she remembered how he'd tried to rein himself in—and how guilty he'd felt when he couldn't. Of course, she'd enjoyed urging him on, had wanted to see what Elijah Turner was like when he threw off all of that restraint. Not only was it gratifying to her that she could have such an effect on him, she figured that was the best way to discover his true personality—when he wasn't closely monitoring everything he said and did. Although he came off as remote, she was beginning to understand that he was actually quite sensitive. He also seemed honest and intrinsically fair.

Her phone rang. Assuming it would be Jill, or maybe Darci, since she was running a few minutes late, she answered using her Bluetooth. "Hello?"

"Cora? It's Aiyana. How are you?"

She froze at the sound of her birth mother's voice. Had Aiyana learned that she and Elijah had spent the night together? Cora had slipped out of his place while it was still dark so that no one would see her. They were both consenting adults; she didn't think what they'd done should be a *really* big deal, at least to anyone else. They did work for the same school, however. So, of course, that would be frowned upon.

Was she about to be confronted about her behavior?

A honk from the car behind her reminded her that it was her turn to clear the intersection. "Um... I'm fine," she said as she gave her SUV some gas. "How are you?"

"Great." Aiyana covered the phone as someone spoke to her in the background. "Sorry about that," she said when she came back on the line. "We just got a new shipment of books for the library."

"From what I've seen, we already have an extensive collection."

"I won't skimp on the library, either."

What *did* she skimp on? Nothing, not when it came to the school. Cora had the impression she worked 24/7 to make sure the boys had everything they could possibly need. "Are you a big reader?"

"I am. I read more nonfiction than anything else, but I stock a lot of action-adventure, sci-fi, mysteries and thrillers for the boys. I encourage them to read by giving them books they're going to like. Feel free to take a look and borrow anything that catches your fancy."

Cora had an e-reader, which was well-stocked, but she didn't say so. She didn't want Aiyana to feel as though her offer wasn't appreciated. "I will. Thank you."

"I hope you'll be able to adjust to living here in Silver Springs," she said. "I know it might require a bit of an adjustment."

"Living out here is…different," Cora admitted. "But it's not without its attractions." She winced as those words came out of her mouth. She thought Aiyana would instantly guess that Elijah was the biggest and brightest of Silver Springs' "attractions," at least where she was concerned. But Aiyana didn't seem to clue in—thank God.

"Your supplies should be in on Monday. I checked, wanted to let you know."

Cora pulled in front of Lolita's Country Kitchen, where Darci had asked to meet for breakfast. She had to admit that it was wonderful to find ample parking—that rarely happened in LA. She wouldn't even have to pay for it. "Wow. How nice of you to follow up."

"No problem. But…that isn't the only reason I called. If you have a minute, I'd like to talk to you about something else."

Oh boy. Maybe she *did* know about Eli. Cora turned off the car but didn't release her seat belt even though she could see Darci waving at her through the window of the diner. "Sure, I've got time. What's going on?"

"One of the other teachers mentioned to me that Doug Maggleby was making you uncomfortable at the pizza parlor last night."

"It wasn't…all that bad," she hedged.

"He was drinking, which I'm sure didn't help. Anyway, I'm sorry. I'll speak to him. I definitely don't want him scaring you off."

"No, don't bother," she said. "He didn't get *too* out of line." Thanks to Eli, he didn't get much of a chance…

"Are you sure?"

"Positive."

"Well, I'll let this incident go, but only because he's had a rough few years. He lost his wife to cancer and is just now getting over it and hoping to find someone else."

"He might have better luck looking for someone closer to his own age," Cora said.

"Yes. If necessary, I'll mention that to him."

"I appreciate your support."

"Of course. That's what I'm here for." She was about to hang up when, impulsively, Cora stopped her.

"Aiyana?"

"Yes?"

"To tell you the truth…" She searched for the right words to express what she had to say and came up empty.

"Have you changed your mind about having me talk to Doug?" Aiyana asked.

"No. This is…something else."

"What is it?"

She tapped her fingers on her steering wheel. "Um… I wanted to make sure you wouldn't be…angry or—or disappointed if I ever…you know…"

"What?" Aiyana prompted.

"Showed interest in your son," she blurted out.

"Elijah?"

Cora squeezed her eyes closed. She had no idea what the heck she was doing. She just hated the feeling that she might be letting Aiyana down by going behind her back, needed to know how serious of an infraction it would be if she were to continue to see Elijah. She had no idea how *he* felt about last night, but she definitely wanted to get to know him better. "Yes. I've seen Gavin but haven't actually met him."

There was a long pause. Afraid of what Aiyana might say to discourage her, Cora hurried to fill the silence. "I realize we both work for you, at the same school, but in the high schools where I've taught, if two teachers happen to go out once in a while, it's pretty much ignored."

"I'm not so concerned about two employees dating…"

"And yet you sound hesitant."

"He bears some unique scars, Cora."

Letting her breath seep out, Cora finally opened her eyes. "I'm aware of that."

"Do you realize that what he's been through will probably always be part of him? How a background like his could affect a relationship?"

Darci was now at the door, watching her with a confused expression, so Cora lifted one finger to indicate she'd be just another minute. "Here's the thing. He's fine the way he is. I'm not asking for anything serious. I think I could be a good friend to him."

More silence. Cora didn't get the impression Aiyana was *against* her seeing Elijah—it was more that she seemed to be weighing certain reservations in her mind, trying to figure out if she should say more.

Cora bit her lip. "I shouldn't have said anything. It wouldn't be serious, like I said. I guess I just…needed to know you wouldn't be too upset if…if we ever hung out."

"I wouldn't be upset. I'm just worried that…well, because he's so hard to get to know, it may not seem as if he can be hurt—"

"Anyone can be hurt."

"*Especially* him," she said. "I guess that's my point. His heart is so big."

"Trust me—it's not like that. You have nothing to worry about."

"Well, if that's the case, no one can have too many

friends," she said, and they both laughed at her quick reversal.

"Okay. Great. Can I ask for one more favor?"

"Of course."

"Don't tell him we had this conversation?"

"Trust me—I won't. He wouldn't like the idea of me getting involved, so to be honest, I'm hoping you won't mention it, either."

"I won't. This will be our little secret. And now I'll let you go."

"Cora?"

She pulled her phone back to her ear. "Yes?"

"Relationships, even friendships, can be unpredictable at times. So protect your own heart, too."

"I will." As Cora disconnected, she felt as if a huge weight had been lifted off her shoulders. Maybe she hadn't come *totally* clean. She wasn't willing to go that far. But at least she knew she wouldn't be doing anything that would upset Aiyana if Aiyana found out about it. As attracted as Cora was to Elijah, she didn't want to kill any chance she had of being part of her biological mother's life—if she ever decided to go for that.

Chapter Eight

"Thanks for being willing to get together," Darci said.

Cora was a little self-conscious about the fact that she hadn't had a chance to shower this morning. When Darci called, she'd rolled out of bed and thrown her hair into a ponytail. She was still tired after being up until the wee hours with Elijah. "I'm glad you reached out," she told Darci.

"I almost didn't, but with school starting on Monday and my kids coming home tomorrow, I figured this would be the best time to get together."

"It's perfect. I haven't had a chance to eat in Silver Springs yet." Cora noted the number of filled tables. "This seems like a popular place."

"It's one of the best cafés in town, not that we have a lot of them," Darci added with a laugh. "Do you know if Elijah got Doug home okay last night?"

Cora took a drink of water from the glass the waitress had delivered to her a moment earlier. "He did. I saw him as he was coming out of Doug's house."

"Did he say anything to you?"

She opened her menu, pretending to be preoccupied by choosing her meal. "Not really." After what Darci had said about the way Elijah was looking at her last night, Cora didn't dare admit to anything. Her face was heating up, threatening to give her away as it was.

Fortunately, someone walked by that Darci knew, drawing her attention. "Hello, Cal!"

"Cal," a handsome, middle-aged man who wore a cowboy hat and boots, stopped, a look of pleasant surprise on his face. "Darci! I didn't even see you there. How are you?"

She got up to give him a hug. "Better. Thanks."

"That ex of yours isn't still giving you trouble, is he?"

"Things seem to have settled down for the moment." She slid back in the booth. "He's met someone else, so that helps."

He shook his head. "You've had a rough year."

"It's been a rough *twelve* years. But the divorce would've been worse without you."

"I didn't do much." He glanced at Cora. "Is this a new friend?"

As Darci introduced them, she told Cora that Cal Buchanon owned a big cattle ranch not far from town. "He supplies New Horizons with beef, gives Aiyana a heck of a deal. Actually, he helps *everyone*," she said emphatically. "Silver Springs wouldn't be what it is without him."

"Stop!" he said, obviously embarrassed. "I do my part, like everyone else. It's very nice to meet you, Cora."

"Likewise," Cora said.

He chatted with Darci for several more minutes before tipping his hat to the both of them and heading to the cashier to pay his bill.

"Cal's superrich," Darci whispered. "And he uses his money to do so much for the community. I was serious when I said Silver Springs wouldn't be the same without him."

"You seem to know him well."

"I do. He has a couple of houses on his ranch that he typically rents to his hands. He let me stay in one *for free* until I could get on my feet. Wouldn't take a dime for six months."

"Is that why you came to Silver Springs? You knew him from before, and he made you that offer, or…"

"No. I came to teach at New Horizons, like you. But the house that was supposed to open up in the faculty housing—the two-bedroom so that I'd have room for my kids—didn't, and I couldn't afford anything in town."

"So how'd you meet him?"

"Through Aiyana. She jumped in to make other arrangements when the faculty housing didn't work out for me."

"How nice of her."

"She's generous, like Cal. And, from what I've heard, Cal has been in love with Aiyana for years, almost since the day she came here. I believe he took me in for her sake. But he's been kind enough to befriend me, too."

"He's never married?"

"Not to my knowledge. He doesn't even date. He's waiting for her."

"He reminds me of Sam Elliott with that gravelly voice and weathered face. Doesn't she care for him in return?"

"I'm convinced she does. The way she looks at him… it's as if he hung the moon. But she's very private about her love life. If you ask her about Cal, she'll make some glib comment about how he's a great guy but she's too old to get married for the first time."

Aiyana was only forty-nine. Cora knew that from the documents provided by the private investigator who'd taken her on pro bono. "Do you ever see them together?"

"I run into them all the time. He supports anything her boys participate in so he comes out to the ranch a lot. And he sends her flowers or chocolates at least once a month. I wish I could find a guy as devoted to me as he is to her," she added wistfully. "My ex only cared about himself."

Cora had no business asking, but she was so curious about her birth mother that she couldn't stop herself. "Do you think they're sleeping together?" she asked, lowering her voice to a whisper.

Darci's mouth twisted as she considered the question. "Don't know, to be honest. When I lived out at his place, she never stayed over, not that I could tell. And I've never known him to sleep at New Horizons. But that doesn't mean it hasn't happened. Like I said, Aiyana's very private about that sort of thing. She'd never let on, even if they were intimate."

"There must be some reason they're not an official couple. What's missing?"

"I couldn't tell you." She made a signal to let Cora know the waitress, who'd introduced herself as Missy, was coming to take their order.

"Sorry to put such an abrupt end to the conversation," she said after she'd ordered pancakes and eggs and Cora had ordered a Spanish omelet. "I was afraid Missy might overhear us. Everyone knows everyone else around here—and even if they don't, most everyone knows Aiyana."

"No problem. I understand."

Difficult though it was, Cora let the conversation drift away from her birth mother to the school and what the coming year would entail. They also discussed some of the more troubled boys.

"How do you deal with those who won't behave?" Cora asked.

"Easy," Darci replied. "I threaten to send them to Elijah."

Cora put down her fork and took a drink of her orange juice. "Why not Aiyana?"

"Elijah tries to spare her anything difficult, anything that might upset or disappoint her. He prefers we get him involved if we need help."

"Elijah's the enforcer."

"Sort of."

"What methods does he use for discipline?"

"The threat of being sent to his office is usually enough. If they do something wrong, they don't want him to find out about it. They care about his good opinion, about getting the chance to be with him for various activities."

"Surely there have been a few who *haven't* cared enough to behave."

"Of course. He barred one boy, Ricky Peterson, from

playing sports and attending the dances and assemblies until he brought up his grades. But then he studied with Ricky for an hour a day. After a few weeks, Ricky was doing better than ever before."

Considering they were talking about a man who called himself a "locked box," Cora thought that was interesting. Apparently, he had plenty of love for the boys—but she'd already noted that when he was on the horseback ride.

She opened her mouth to ask if Darci had ever heard anything about the various women Elijah had been with but caught herself. She couldn't show that much interest, didn't want to give Darci any indication that there was something going on between them. Since they weren't serious, she preferred to keep it on the down low. So she asked about Darci's marriage and divorce, and then she tried to offer some support. But in the back of her mind she couldn't quit thinking about Elijah and the role he played on the ranch. Aiyana remained on her mind, as well. Her biological mother was such an enigma. Why wouldn't she marry Cal?

Cora had just stepped out of the shower when she heard a knock at the door. Assuming it was Doug, since he'd caught her when she got back from breakfast to say he had some fresh vegetables he planned to gather from his garden and bring over, she groaned and started to grab some clothes so that she could get dressed. Then she realized she'd have a much better excuse not to invite him in if she answered in her robe.

Prepared to thank him and quickly send him on his way, she pasted a smile on her face and cracked open the door. But it wasn't her neighbor, it was Elijah. He stood on her stoop in a pair of faded jeans, his tan, muscular arms stretching the sleeves of his red New Horizons T-shirt as he tossed his keys from hand to hand.

"Hello," she said, blinking in surprise.

His gaze lowered to her robe. "Just getting up?"

"No. I met Darci in town for breakfast and didn't have time to get ready beforehand, so I just showered." She'd also done a conditioning treatment on her hair, given herself a mani-pedi and rubbed her whole body with some vanilla-scented lotion. She told herself she wanted to look and feel her best to start her new job, that she was doing this as a matter of routine. But she knew Elijah had more to do with it than she cared to admit.

His lips curved into a devilish smile. "Then I'd say my timing is perfect."

Not only was he smiling freely, he was smiling at *her*. "For…"

"I owe you a little something, remember?"

Slightly concerned by how easily he could make her knees weak, since she was supposed to be keeping some emotional distance in this relationship, Cora drew a steadying breath. "You don't owe me anything."

He reached out and tugged on her belt to loosen it, so she stepped back to let him inside. The last thing she needed was for someone to drive by and see them. "You don't think it's too risky to come to my house during the day? If you're not careful the whole school will be talking about us."

"What do you mean? It's much safer to come during the day. Then it doesn't look like we're trying to hide anything."

That made sense, but the fact that her robe was coming open also made it difficult to think. He continued to pull on her belt—slowly so she'd have time to stop him if she wanted. But she didn't stop him, and soon the belt fell to the ground.

Suddenly nervous, she wet her lips as she stared up at him. "So now it's my turn, huh?"

"Unless you have other plans for the next hour or so…"

Cora felt she should come up with something. Put this off, at least until she could regain her perspective. She shouldn't be this excited.

On the other hand, she'd just spent two hours getting ready to see him—and here he was.

Dipping his head, he kissed her long and slow as he slid his big hands inside her robe and gripped her waist.

He wasn't holding back today. Last night had convinced him that she wasn't skittish, wasn't going to bail out too easily. "I take it you don't want to…to talk first," she said.

"No. I'm not interested in talking."

Cora found it quite erotic that she was naked while he was fully dressed. She also liked his level of focus. "So there'd be no point in putting on my clothes."

"Why make me take them off again?" He hoisted her up onto the dining table, putting her on her back.

She caught the lapels of her robe so it wouldn't fall *completely* open. The soft terry cloth was beginning to feel like a safety blanket. But he pulled the fabric out of her grasp and ran his fingers over her bare stomach and breasts.

Cora shuddered as a ripple of pleasure went through her.

"You like that?" He continued his light touch, skimming up her neck to her face, where he ran his thumb over her bottom lip. "You're so beautiful."

The compliment surprised her. He wasn't much for that sort of thing. She told herself not to take him too seriously, but at the same time she caught his hand and pulled his thumb into her mouth.

His pupils flared as her tongue moved over his skin, and he lowered his mouth to her breast.

Every nerve seemed to fire at once; she'd never been more aroused.

"Now I see how convenient a Brazilian makes everything," he said as his mouth moved down her stomach. "Easy access. I like that."

Cora couldn't even speak. His hands were on her hips, and he was pulling her toward him, spreading her legs so he could fit between her knees. "Maybe…maybe we should wait until we know each other better for this," she said, finding her voice.

"Because…"

"Because it…it makes me *really* self-conscious."

"You don't have to be self-conscious with me."

He bent his head. When she felt his tongue, she nearly jumped off the table.

"It's okay," he murmured, his breath warm. "Relax. This is going to be fun."

The next few minutes were more than fun; they were mind-blowing. Cora drew in a deep breath and closed her eyes as he used his mouth in a way she'd never experienced before. The sucking motion was so subtle, so gentle and so incredibly effective that her legs began to quiver. She felt his hand rub one of them, as if in encouragement, before that hand slid back up to her breast.

She was seconds away from the best climax of her life. Cora felt the escalation, the compulsion of her body to reach that pinnacle.

Then the doorbell rang.

Trying to force her sluggish brain to work as it usually did, she started to get up. She thought Elijah would stop so she could deal with her guest, especially because his truck was outside. They couldn't be caught doing something like this. It wouldn't look good. But he muttered a gruff, "No!" and held her that much more tightly as he continued his ministrations.

He was so insistent that she let her head fall back and reached for the sides of the table. She had to hold on to something…

"Cora, you there?"

Doug. Of course. He *would* show up at the worst possible moment.

"The door!" she whispered emphatically, but Elijah wouldn't let Doug take this away from her. She felt his beard growth on her thighs as he shook his head in refusal.

Fortunately, the climax she'd been chasing burst upon her soon after, despite the fact that Doug knocked again.

After Elijah heard her gasp and felt her body jerk, he straightened in satisfaction. He'd given her one hell of a climax. She could tell that had been his goal, but he didn't seem pleased. "Damn him," he grumbled, his voice low as he scooped her off the table, set her on her feet and bent to retrieve the belt to her robe.

"What should we do?" Her mind scrambled to decide how best to explain Elijah's presence, her disheveled appearance and their delay.

After a brief hesitation, he took charge. "She's in the shower," he called out, turning her toward the bedroom and giving her a little push.

As she hurried down the hall, he headed for the door.

"When I got here, she yelled for me to come in," she heard him say as soon as she was safely behind the closed door of her bedroom. "But I've been waiting for fifteen minutes, and she's not out yet. So you might want to leave those here or come back later. I'm going to come back myself."

Doug said something in reply. Cora couldn't make it out. His voice wasn't as strident as Elijah's. Then there was silence, and when she peeked out, they were both gone.

Smooth move, she texted to Elijah.

What I did with Doug or before? came his response.

Although she could tell he was teasing, his words let her know he was still very much fixated on what had occurred—and she couldn't blame him. She was having a hard time forgetting about it herself, and she was the one who'd at least been satisfied. Pretty proud of yourself, huh?

That felt good—even to me.

Lol. I won't lie. You could win an award with that technique.

Glad to hear it. Then maybe you'll see me again tonight.

She could only imagine how aroused he'd been when he'd had to leave. Being interrupted at that point was never fun. But she wasn't sure they should continue what they'd started. She'd been thinking of this fling in such a harmless way. She'd presented seeing Elijah to Aiyana in a harmless way. And yet…spending more time with him was beginning to feel dangerous.

Can't. Going to LA to see my folks.

Until that moment, she hadn't planned on returning home. She was essentially running away. But she knew where she'd spend the night if she didn't get out of Silver Springs, and she needed to put on the brakes, gain some perspective, rethink what they were doing. The tenderness she felt at any thought of him frightened her. This wasn't nearly as casual as she'd imagined.

When will you be back?

Tomorrow night.

Call me when you get in.

Okay, she wrote back. But she didn't return until it was late—too late to consider seeing him before school started the following morning.

Chapter Nine

Eli had never had trouble concentrating. Not since he'd overcome what he'd been through as a child and grown into an adult. He was so focused on his job and the boys he served that there were days when he almost forgot to eat. Work was what he enjoyed, what kept him going and looking forward to each new day. He was especially busy this time of year, when there was so much to do in order to get the semester started off right.

On top of that, his two youngest brothers were back, and Dallas, the middle brother who'd taken them climbing in Yosemite, was temporarily visiting. The following week, Eli spent most of his evenings with them, which he enjoyed, but he often found his mind drifting when it shouldn't. He kept remembering what it had been like to make love to Cora, felt such a strong craving to be with her again he couldn't help watching for her whenever he was on campus. She'd texted him when she left LA last Sunday night but only to let him know she'd be getting back too late to see him. With Dallas in town, Eli hadn't thought much of it. He'd told her to let him know when she'd be available, which indicated he wanted to see her again, but he hadn't heard from her in six days. He wasn't sure what she was thinking. Although she'd smile and wave if she happened to bump into him—she wasn't *un*friendly—she'd turn away right after, wouldn't really meet his eyes. And she never called him or reached out to him, even at night. Since Dallas was staying at the big house with Aiyana, Liam and Bentley, they *could've* seen each other despite Dallas's presence on the ranch, if she'd acted interested.

Eli had almost stopped by her place a dozen times. He would have at least called her, but he could tell that something was different. She'd withdrawn. He wanted to believe she was just busy. Being a new teacher, *any* teacher, the first week of school was stressful. He needed to give her time to settle in, couldn't expect to take priority over her work. From what he could tell, she was dedicated to her students and intent on getting to know them. Since he was the one who'd hired her, and he'd chosen her over a candidate most others had expected to get the job, he wanted her to excel. He'd heard from several of the boys that she was already well liked, which gave him hope. But when he saw her at their first football game last night, and she still didn't reach out to him afterward, like he'd thought she might with the weekend before them, he knew it was more than her job that was keeping her away.

She'd decided she wouldn't see him again. Why? What had made her change her mind? Had she decided a strictly physical relationship wasn't worth it? Had she gotten back with her boyfriend? Or…what?

"Hey, where are you tonight, man?"

Eli blinked and drew his attention back to Dallas and Gavin, who'd dragged him to the bar. He didn't come here often, was careful about how much he drank. Although drinking could wipe out the painful thoughts and memories that plagued him, it could also rob him of his functionality. And he was determined to show the boys he worked with how to overcome that temptation, not fall right into it.

"Sorry, what'd you say?" he asked Dallas, who'd broken into his thoughts.

Dallas finished his last swallow of beer. "You're a million miles away. I was wondering what you were thinking."

Eli lifted his own glass. "I'm thinking Freddy Nance deserves to play ahead of Jason Peachtree."

"Do you have any idea what the heck he's talking about?" Dallas looked to Gavin for an explanation.

"Cougar football," Gavin replied. "Freddy and Jason are both hoping to make first-string quarterback at New Horizons."

"Jason's so gifted," Eli said. "But Freddy's willing to work twice as hard. That counts for more, in my book."

Dallas shook his head. "I swear, big brother. You need to get off that campus a little more often. Look at the chicks here, man. Have some fun."

Dallas's childhood hadn't been any better than Elijah's. After a relatively normal life, he'd watched his father come unhinged and shoot his mother and his sister, and attempt to shoot him before he managed to run out of the house. When the police came, they found that his father had turned the gun on himself. While Eli used work to anesthetize him from his past, Dallas deadened the painful memories he carried with sex when he wasn't climbing and adrenaline when he was. Eli was fairly certain, of the three of them, Aiyana worried about him the most. Eli did, too. Although Gavin had been abandoned at six years old in a park, he seemed to cope better with life.

Or maybe he just pretended to.

"I try to leave the women alone," Eli said.

"Because..."

"Because I'll wreck their life. I should come with a warning label."

"It's only sex, man. As long as it's consensual and doesn't get too crazy, sex never hurt anybody."

"You forget," Eli said drily. "This is a small town. There's no way not to run into the same woman over and over."

"You can't do that sort of thing here," Gavin grumbled in agreement.

"Then you *both* need to get off that ranch a little more often. Drive to LA."

"If we slept with as many women as you do—" Gavin started, but Dallas cut him off.

"You'd have some fun for a change."

Eli rolled his eyes. "Or wind up with a disease."

"Not if you're careful."

"I don't get the impression you're as careful as you should be—about anything," Eli joked, but if Dallas answered, he didn't hear it. He felt his smile wilt the second he glanced up and saw Cora walk into the bar with Darci Spinoza.

She didn't notice him, not at first. But it didn't take long. Those wide, innocent eyes of hers, busy scanning the tables along the periphery of the dance floor as she looked for a place where they could sit down, stopped the second they encountered him—and recognition dawned.

To her credit, she and Darci walked over to say hello. Actually, Cora didn't really have any choice—neither one of them did. He was their boss, after all. It would've been rude to ignore him.

Fortunately, Darci didn't seem to know anything had ever happened between him and Cora. "Hey." She grinned at Dallas. "Look who's in town—trouble!"

"You know me already," Dallas responded. "It's great to see you again. You're Darci, right? The English teacher?"

They'd met at the school Christmas party. Aiyana insisted that the entire family get together for the holidays—no matter what they had going.

"Yes," Darci replied. "It's great to see you, too."

Dallas slid off his stool and stood, his gaze shifting to Cora. Eli could tell he found her attractive. "I don't believe I've ever seen *you* before."

"I noticed you at the football game last night, down on the field with Eli."

"If only I would've known *you'd* be in the stands," he said.

Darci introduced Cora, and Cora smiled politely as she

shook first with Dallas and then Gavin. "Nice to meet you both."

"You must know Eli," Dallas said.

"Yes. Eli hired me."

"I can see why." Dallas pulled over a stool and began looking for a second one. "Any chance you'd like to join us?"

Cora started to decline. She looked as though she couldn't get away fast enough. But Darci didn't seem to be paying any attention to her discomfort. She overrode Cora's response with an eager, "Sure. Why not? We were looking for some entertainment."

Gavin pulled over another chair while Dallas gave her a bow. "We're happy to provide that, aren't we, boys?"

Darci took the seat closest to Dallas, which left the stool between Eli and Gavin for Cora. She sat down, but Eli got the impression she was being careful not to touch him, even incidentally.

Darci and Cora ordered a drink. Then they all talked for an hour—about Dallas's climbing, the places he'd visited, that he'd be leaving in three days, the fact that Seth, another brother who was a sculptor, had secured a gallery showing in San Francisco, one he'd been working hard to parlay into a second and third showing in Chicago and New York, which was why he hadn't visited this summer as he'd originally intended.

Darci brought up her kids and her divorce and how much better she was feeling now that she was getting beyond it, but Cora didn't say much. She mostly listened—and focused on Dallas or Gavin, anyone but him. When Dallas asked her to dance, she agreed, but Eli had a difficult time watching. He didn't care to consider the reason.

Eventually, while they were having a second drink, she mumbled something about having to go to the bathroom and crossed to the far side of the bar, where the restrooms were located. Eli held off for a few seconds, so it wouldn't appear as if they were going together. Then he followed her and waited in the hallway until she came out.

She took one look at him and stopped.

"Have I done something to offend you?" he asked.

"Of course not."

"Then why haven't I heard from you?"

"No reason," she said. "I've been…busy. I figured you were, too."

He shoved a hand through his hair. He was so confused by her abrupt reversal. "You didn't get back with your boyfriend when you went to LA last weekend…"

She shook her head. "Didn't even see him. I went to my folks'."

"So…what is it?" he asked. "*Something*'s different."

"Nothing. Not really. I just… I think you were right."

A trickle of foreboding went through him. "About…"

"You're my boss. It isn't wise to get so intimately…*involved* when we work together."

That wasn't the reason she'd stepped back; he could tell. "So… I screwed up somehow. You don't want to see me anymore."

She rubbed her forehead. "You didn't screw up."

"I must've done something, because I thought everything went…well. Better than well. *Great*." He lowered his voice in case someone else happened upon them. "Maybe I came too soon that first time and disappointed you, and you have every right to be frustrated that I wouldn't be more sensitive to *your* pleasure, but I hadn't been with anyone in a long time. That isn't how I usually behave. Trust me. I'll make sure it doesn't happen again."

"I'm not like that, Eli. I *wanted* you to come—to do whatever you were compelled to do. That first time has nothing to do with it."

"Then there's something else…"

She said nothing, so he stepped closer.

"I'd really appreciate it if you'd take two seconds to explain, so I don't have to keep wondering why everything was fine and then..."

After tucking her hair behind her ears, she lifted her chin to confront him. "Being with you *did* go well. *Too* well. Every night before I go to sleep, you're all I can think about—the way you touched me, the way you kissed me. Even the way you *smell*."

"So why are you stonewalling me?" he asked, stunned.

"I'm trying to do us both a favor, okay?"

He spread out his hands. "By rejecting me?"

"By adhering to our original agreement! You wanted to keep it strictly physical."

"So did you!"

"Yes, but—"

"Physical means we touch each other."

"Except I *feel* something! I know it's crazy. We just met. But you were right in the beginning. I can't do it," she said and brushed past him.

Cora wished she could go home. Sitting next to Eli, talking and laughing with his brothers, certainly didn't make her want him any less. She'd thought her admission in the hallway would scare him away, or at least make her feel so exposed *that* would douse the flames. But the way he watched her only made her crave his hands on her body more with each passing second. Sexual energy all but crackled through the air between them like electricity.

How could she become infatuated with someone so quickly? Especially when she'd only ever been lukewarm with her previous partners?

Her ex-boyfriend would've given *anything* to be able to make her feel even half as much...

Her response to Eli was a mystery—an ironic mystery. After being so cavalier with him that night when he brought Doug home, she was getting what she deserved, having to eat her words. And, to make it all worse, she couldn't slip out of the bar to escape the tension between her and the man sitting next to her. Forcing Darci to leave when she was having so much fun would be too selfish. After what Darci had been through, this was the kind of thing she needed. A night that was carefree and fun. The chance to talk and laugh and forget the difficulties of the past year. Darci was enjoying every moment and didn't seem to notice that Cora sat on pins and needles.

"Dance with me."

Dallas had danced with her twice before, but this was Eli. He hadn't danced with anyone yet, and because he'd asked in front of his brothers, she didn't feel as if she could refuse him.

"Go dance!" Darci said before she could respond, and she got up and let him lead her onto the floor.

Rihanna's "Stay" was playing as he looped his arms around her back. She tried to resist getting too close but gave up on that the moment his hands slid up her back. He was coaxing her to relax, which made it impossible to resist the temptation to melt into him.

"Why are you doing this?" she asked as they swayed to the music.

"Why am I doing what?"

His breath was warm against her ear. "Tempting fate."

"Because it's too late to back away now. We're already in this."

"It's not too late."

As he brought his head up, his lips brushed her neck. To the casual observer that move probably looked inadvertent, but *she* understood he'd done it on purpose—and felt a corresponding sizzle zip through her.

"You think we're going to be able to fight what we feel for a whole year?" he murmured.

What else could they do? He was Aiyana's son! The only reason she'd let herself go as far as she did was because she'd assumed she'd be able to remain somewhat objective. Now that she'd spent some time with him, however, she had to acknowledge that it wasn't going to be easy come, easy go.

"We can try."

"As far as I'm concerned that'll be a frustrating exercise in futility," he said. "I'm already going crazy."

She hated that she'd started something and was refusing to finish it. That didn't seem quite fair. Maybe she needed to let this play out. She'd never gotten involved in a relationship that was more physical than anything else. That meant the attraction might be explosive at first, but would eventually burn itself out, didn't it?

If so, she was worried about nothing.

"To be honest, so am I," she admitted. "So…where can we go?"

"You mean later? What's wrong with my place?"

"I mean *now*," she told him.

He pulled back to look at her. "Are you serious?"

She could already taste his kiss, had committed every detail about him to memory. "Do you have a problem with that?"

"Absolutely not," he replied. "Make your way out back. There's a side patio where smokers go that should be fairly deserted. I'll be there in a few."

Since they didn't want to be caught together, this was a risky endeavor. That she was willing to take such a gamble surprised Cora. It wasn't like her. But nothing she'd done with Elijah so far had been like her and, in this instance, the need for privacy couldn't outweigh the urgency to feel him inside her. After battling that desire for a whole week, she was more than ready to surrender.

When Eli returned to the table, Darci looked up at him in surprise. "Where's Cora?"

"She went to the bathroom."

"Again?"

He shrugged as if he hadn't asked for details, and, as soon as she was distracted by something Dallas said, he nudged Gavin. "Why don't you ask Darci to dance?" he murmured.

Gavin seemed startled by this atypical request, but Eli had spoken low and used a tone that suggested he not question it, and Gavin didn't.

As soon as Gavin and Darci walked away, Eli leaned close to Dallas. "I'm going out back," he said. "Keep Darci occupied, will ya?"

"Keep her occupied?" Dallas repeated.

"Make sure she doesn't go looking for Cora."

Dallas sat up straight. "What are you two going to be doing?"

When Eli didn't answer, his brother swore under his breath. "No way! I've been flirting with her all night, with zero results. You dance with her once, and she goes outside with you?"

"It's not like that," he said.

"Then what's it like?"

Eli lifted his beer. "None of your business. Just take care of Darci, okay?"

"Sure. What are brothers for?" he replied. "But isn't Cora your new art teacher? Is that okay? Because I'll step in for you if it isn't," he joked.

"Like hell you will," Eli grumbled and tossed back what was left in his glass before making his way to the door leading to the patio and the parking lot beyond.

Cora was waiting for him near the vine-covered trellis. Two guys were smoking on the far side of the patio, but they were so deep in conversation they weren't paying any attention. Taking Cora's hand, he quietly led her to the back of the building, which faced nothing except a wide expanse of farmland.

"On second thought, maybe this is a little reckless," she said as he pressed her up against the building.

It had taken him long enough to join her that she'd grown nervous. He could tell. "Apparently, you need a little recklessness in your life."

"Because…"

He kissed his way up her neck. "It's exciting."

"Being reckless is a good way to get burned."

Threading his fingers through hers, he held her hands above her head. "Like I said, we're in it now."

"And if someone comes out?"

"They won't."

"How do you know?"

"I told my brothers to see to it."

Her eyes widened. "You did *what*?"

"I didn't want you to worry about Darci."

"But…what must your brothers think?"

"It doesn't matter."

"It does to me!" she said. "I'm embarrassed!"

"I'm sorry. It was either that or risk having Darci come looking for you. I figured that would be *more* embarrassing, and I knew I could trust my brothers to make sure that didn't happen."

He was afraid she was going to leave. He held his breath as she stared up at him, and bit back a curse when she pulled away. But after taking a few steps, she turned back and grabbed him by the shirtfront, pulling him up against her again. "This is crazy. Look at us! We're behind a *bar*. And somehow that's not enough to stop me. What you told your brothers isn't enough to stop me, either. Because I've never wanted anyone like I want you."

He let his breath go in relief. "Hallelujah. Then I suggest you relax," he said and slid his hand up her skirt.

* * *

Cora told herself that she should care more about the fact that Dallas and Gavin knew what was going on—and that Darci could easily figure it out. But the kiss Elijah gave her was so achingly sweet that the last thing she wanted to do was walk away. This was a new side of him, one she hadn't seen before.

"I *love* the way you touch me." She'd anticipated coming together in the same heady rush they'd experienced before. They'd both felt the same chemistry on the dance floor. But tonight Eli was taking his time.

"Then you needed this reminder. Maybe it means you won't ignore me this week."

"You could've called *me*," she said as his mouth found her earlobe.

"I was getting signals that precluded that."

"I don't remember sending any signals."

"You wouldn't even look at me."

"Because I knew where it would lead."

"To this."

"Yes."

"Is that a problem?"

She sighed as he kissed her again. "It doesn't feel like one right now."

His fingers hooked the thin fabric of her thong and began sliding it down her legs. "Why hold back? Like I told you before, I'll give you whatever you ask for."

Except his heart. He'd made that clear. But, considering the situation, did it really matter? She was only here for the year. And once he found out she was Aiyana's daughter—if she ever decided to tell him—she couldn't imagine he'd be pleased that she'd allowed them to get so intimate without disclosing her true identity.

"Great. Then give me this," she said and undid his pants.

Chapter Ten

Cora had never had sex outside of a bar or any other public place. She'd heard of other women doing things like that, but she'd never dreamed *she'd* be one of them. It was humbling to learn she could be that girl, but…what'd changed? What'd made her do such a thing?

It was Eli. He had such a profound effect on her. That animal magnetism, the immediacy of what they'd done, had been potent. She'd been so aroused, so sensitive to his every touch that she'd been able to climax when he did, making the fifteen minutes they spent outside quite an experience. She'd never forget him holding her up against the building, the moon full overhead as he drove into her, the only sound she could hear above the music filtering out of the building that of their own labored breathing—and then her groan at the end, which he'd quickly smothered with another kiss.

She was having a torrid affair—with her boss. Her ex-boyfriend would be shocked. Her parents would be shocked. Heck, *she* was shocked. She and Eli hadn't even used a condom. They hadn't had one, hadn't come prepared because they hadn't expected anything to happen. They'd been forced to use the withdrawal method.

"Where've you been?" Darci asked once Cora had righted her skirt, smoothed down her hair and returned to the table.

Cora hoped it was too dark to see the blush heating her cheeks. "It's so hot in here." She slid over as Eli joined them. He'd purposely let her go in first so that they wouldn't come back at the same time. "I stepped out for some fresh air, and there were a couple of guys outside, smoking. We got into a conversation."

"Oh. You were gone so long I was about to come looking for you." She lifted her glass to catch the attention of the waitress.

Fortunately, Darci didn't seem suspicious, but Dallas wasn't about to let Cora off quite that easily. "Wasn't it every bit as hot outside?" he asked with a grin that left little question he was messing with her.

Eli shot his brother a warning glance, but there was nothing he could do or say in front of Darci, who turned to look at her in expectation of her response.

"It was…a little warm," Cora said, but the waitress Darci had called over appeared. As soon as Darci turned to speak with her, Cora leaned closer to Dallas. "Actually, after it was all over, I could've used a cigarette myself!"

Dallas burst out laughing and slapped his older brother on the back. "Damn, I like her. She's *definitely* hooking up with the wrong Turner."

"What'd you say?" Darci asked as the waitress left. "Something Turner?"

Dallas clinked his glass against Cora's. "Not Turner, *learner*. I said Cora's a fast learner."

Darci blinked in apparent confusion. "What'd you learn?" she asked Cora but Eli dragged Cora onto the dance floor to save her from answering.

Cora was fairly certain she'd never had more fun. On some level, she knew she was screwing up her life. She was so taken with Eli, too taken for it to be safe. But she could hardly feel bad about what she was doing when she was still in the middle of it. She, Darci and the Turner boys talked, laughed and danced until the bar closed. Then Eli drove them all home, since he'd had much less to drink— barely two beers. Although Cora wasn't much of a drinker herself, she'd been feeling more carefree than usual. After her stint outside with Eli, she'd quit holding back and simply cut loose. If she was going to regret this night, she figured she might as well go all the way.

Eli dropped Darci and Gavin off first, since they both lived in town. Cora would have to reclaim her SUV in the morning, but she was so happy and tired when she got home that she wasn't worried about that or anything else.

After Eli pulled into her driveway, he walked her to the door. Dallas was probably watching from the truck as he kissed her, but she didn't care about that any more than anything else tonight—and just to prove it, she pulled Eli back and kissed him a second time before letting him go. "You are *so* hot!" she said.

"And you are so drunk," he responded with a laugh.

"I'm not drunk. I mean…not *that* drunk."

"Yeah, you are."

"I'll never forget tonight."

A thoughtful expression claimed his face as his gaze moved over her. "Neither will I," he said. "But you'd better go inside if you don't want your neighbors peering out to see what you're up to."

She let him go, but once she was inside, she twirled around the living room, reliving the evening before falling onto her bed. "What a night," she said aloud. She thought Eli might come back after he took Dallas to Aiyana's. She wanted him to. But if he tried to knock, she didn't hear it. She fell asleep before she could even take off her clothes, and when she woke up, it was late morning.

Reluctant to roll out of bed, she checked her phone— and found she'd missed several calls since she'd paid any attention to that sort of thing last, which was before she'd gone to the bar. Her brother. Her mother. Jill. She'd even missed a call from Aiyana.

Expecting a nasty headache to hit as soon as she sat up,

she moved gingerly at first, but she wasn't as hungover as she'd thought she might be. She deserved worse.

With a yawn, she shoved her hair out of her face and put her phone on speaker so she could listen to her messages with minimum effort while sitting on the bed.

Her mom: "Call me when you get a chance, honey. I found the cutest dress for your birthday, but it's expensive so I'd like you to try it on before I buy it. When will you be coming home?"

Cora smiled in affection. Her birthday wasn't for six months, but her mother bought her stuff all year long.

Her brother: "Just calling to see how my baby sister's doing. I'll be in New York for a few weeks trying to line up the financing for my next film, so don't panic if you don't hear from me. I'll check in when I get back."

She hated that she'd missed his call. Ashton was always so busy these days.

Jill: "So how's Silver Springs? I was hoping to come visit you next weekend, like we talked about, but Todd's grandmother will be celebrating her ninetieth birthday in Palm Springs, and he wants me to go with him. Give me a call so we can set another date."

She'd never told Jill that she'd slept with Eli. She'd decided it didn't make sense to tell anyone since she wasn't going to be with him again.

So much for that…

Aiyana: "Hi, Cora. Sorry for the late notice, but I was wondering if you'd be able to join the boys and me for dinner tomorrow. I'd love the opportunity to get to know you better."

Cora hungered for the opportunity to get to know her better, too. But by boys, did Aiyana mean Eli and possibly Gavin and Dallas? Or was she talking strictly about the two youngest Turners—the ones living at home?

Cora sighed as she stared at her phone. She hesitated

to put Eli in an awkward situation by showing up at his family dinner, but... Aiyana was the whole reason she'd come to Silver Springs. She wanted to accept the invitation.

After mulling it over, she texted him. Your mother has invited me to dinner today. Will you be there?

His response came almost right away. Yes.

Is it okay if I accept?

Why wouldn't it be?

Because she wouldn't be attending in the capacity they thought—as merely a new teacher at the ranch. She was excited to see how Aiyana lived, felt Aiyana's house and the items in it might reveal more about who her biological mother was and what her life had been like. At a minimum, she'd probably be treated to pictures of her grandparents and uncles, maybe even some of the places Aiyana had lived in the past.

But Eli didn't know that her interest extended beyond what she'd stated in her interview.

I don't want to intrude on your time with your family.

You won't be intruding.

She thought he'd leave it at that, but he texted her again a few minutes later.

When do you want to get your car?

In an hour or so? I was about to take a shower.

No problem. I can wait.

She put her phone on the nightstand only to hear it signal another text.

This was from Eli, too: Better yet, why don't I join you?

Aiyana must've said something to Doug Maggleby, even though she'd said she wouldn't, because he'd been less intrusive the past week. Or maybe he was getting the hint. Regardless, Cora was relieved that Doug wasn't there hoping to talk to her every time she walked out her front door, but she still didn't want him to see Eli's truck sitting outside. You can't park in front. We'll have to be more careful or people are going to get the wrong idea.

You mean they might get the right idea.

She couldn't help laughing. Basically.

Well, we can't have that. I'll walk over and slip in. No one will see me.

Oh boy. She was about to sink even further into her "torrid affair." But there wasn't a darn thing she could do about it. Even if she said no now, she knew she'd say yes later.

I'll leave the back door unlocked.

"Damn, I'm glad I hired you," Eli joked as they dropped onto her bed after thirty minutes of the best shower sex she'd ever had. "But since we seem to make love in a vertical position more often than not, I'd better spend more time at the gym. My arms feel like they're about to fall off."

She leaned on one elbow so she could smile down at him. "You didn't seem to be struggling."

"Are you kidding? You weigh a ton."

The twinkle in his eye confirmed that he was teasing

her. "You said you like my body! You said it was the hottest body you've ever seen."

"Heat of the moment," he scoffed, but one finger traced her breast as if he'd meant every word.

"Fine." She knocked his hand away. "I guess I'll have to find someone who's more…appreciative of my physical appearance."

In a quick, easy motion, he rolled her onto her back, straddled her hips and pinned her arms above her head. "No way. You're mine for the entire year, remember? And I plan to make the most of it."

He'd already proved that… "Do you think we're really going to be able to pull this off?" she asked. "Without people finding out, I mean? Without it turning into a big deal that…that comes to the attention of your mother?"

He bent his head to nuzzle her neck. "No doubt there will be talk."

"You're not concerned?"

Slowly, he kissed his way up to her mouth. "Not concerned enough to stay away."

"So what do you propose we do?"

"Ignore it. As long as we're both performing at our jobs, we shouldn't have any problem."

"Maybe I should go on the pill…"

He lifted his head at her abrupt change of subject. "Would you mind? I'm willing to be responsible for birth control, but I admit I'd love to be able to come inside you."

She hated the way her heart seemed to beat in double time as she gazed up at him. She was getting in too deep. He'd told her he wasn't capable of opening up, of making her feel loved and validated.

Was she about to learn what his other girlfriends had learned?

"Cora? Would you mind?" he repeated eagerly.

She drew a bolstering breath. "No."

* * *

A bead of sweat rolled down between Cora's shoulder blades as she stood on the wraparound porch of the large, two-story ranch house that belonged to Aiyana. A gusty breeze tossed her hair around, and she'd worn a light, flowery sundress, so she wasn't overly warm; she was battling nerves.

"Relax," she muttered as she knocked. She'd seen Aiyana's home before, from a distance. Although built on the periphery of the ranch, it wasn't far from the administration building.

Aiyana answered the door. Eli's truck was already in the drive. Cora saw him the moment Aiyana showed her in, but she barely allowed her glance to skim over him as Aiyana introduced her to Dallas and Gavin, both of whom she'd met, of course, and Liam and Bentley. Cora had Liam as a student in one of her classes, so she was familiar with him, too. A tall, gangly boy with a bit of acne, he excelled in basketball, from what she'd heard. She'd only ever seen Bentley, who was African American, on the football field.

She handed the wine she'd brought to Aiyana as she said hello to everyone else.

Eli offered to pour her a drink, but she declined. After imbibing so much at the bar last night, she wasn't interested in more alcohol. She accepted a bottle of water instead while listening to Liam complain about how much trouble he was having with the self-portrait he'd been assigned in her class. After some small talk with the others, she went up to his room to help with it while Aiyana put the finishing touches on dinner.

Leaving the kitchen and dining area gave Cora a chance to see more of the house. As she would've expected, every room was clean and tastefully decorated. Aiyana had pictures of her boys all over the place—senior portraits, family portraits and candid shots from their various sports. She saw a few of Eli. Like Bentley, he'd played football. But it wasn't until after she'd helped Liam and set him to finishing the rest of the assignment on his own that she was able to look over those pictures more carefully.

She wandered down the hall, eventually winding up in the living room. She could hear Aiyana banging around in the kitchen and the boys watching TV in the great room but wasn't in any hurry to return to the group, especially when she spotted the family photograph she'd been hoping to see of Aiyana with her parents and brothers. It was framed and sitting on an old 1960s piano.

She'd just picked up that picture when she heard someone come into the room behind her.

She turned to see Eli.

"You're all finished with Liam?"

"I am. He's still upstairs working, but I figured I should make him do as much as possible." She almost put down the photograph. She felt guilty snooping around but was too curious about the people in that photograph, and her connection to them, not to take advantage of the opportunity. "These are your grandparents?" she asked, indicating the couple in the middle.

"Yeah. Hank and Consuelo."

"Your mother mentioned that Consuelo is a Nicaraguan immigrant."

"That's true. She had one son when her husband left her to come to America. He promised he'd make a better life, then send for them."

"And?"

"She never heard from him again."

Cora felt her jaw drop. "He moved on without her?"

"He was killed trying to swim across the Rio Grande to reach Texas. She came looking for him as soon as she could cobble together the money. But she couldn't find him. It was two years before she learned what happened. By then she was living in a small shack on Hank's farm with her son—German, who was six at the time—picking fruit."

"And Hank fell in love with her?"

"Eventually. Consuelo married two other guys first, Aiyana's father, who was an abusive jerk, and another man with whom she had her last two boys. That didn't work out, either. He walked out on her or something."

"Then she married Hank. So Hank's her fourth husband?"

A fond smile curved Eli's lips. "Yes. She finally got it right."

"How'd they get together?"

"He says he fell in love with her cooking first. Her third husband wouldn't pay his child support, so, to get by, she'd make homemade tortillas and tamales to sell on the weekends. Hank would come to her stand first thing Sunday morning, which was her only day off, and buy almost everything she had."

"Wow. He *must've* loved her cooking."

"That wasn't all there was to it. He couldn't have eaten that many tortillas and tamales. Once they started dating, she found he had a whole freezer full."

Cora laughed. "What a story!"

"I've never seen a man adore a woman more than Hank adores Consuelo."

His wistful expression caught Cora's attention. He loved them almost as much as Aiyana. "So…these three must be your mother's brothers." She pointed at the other men in the photograph.

"Yes." He fingered the one with the darkest skin. "None of the children actually belong to Hank, but he claims them all and loves them as if they do."

For which they should all be so grateful. Eli didn't state that, but the subtext was clear, and that subtext made it difficult for Cora not to bristle. She'd heard a lot of that

YOUR PARTICIPATION IS REQUESTED!

Dear Reader,

Since you are a lover of our books – we would like to get to know you!

Inside you will find a short Reader's Survey. Sharing your answers with us will help our editorial staff understand who you are and what activities you enjoy.

To thank you for your participation, we would like to send you 2 books and 2 gifts – **ABSOLUTELY FREE!**

Enjoy your gifts with our appreciation,

Pam Powers

SEE INSIDE FOR READER'S SURVEY

For Your Reading Pleasure...

We'll send you 2 books and 2 gifts
ABSOLUTELY FREE
just for completing our Reader's Survey!

Visit us at:
www.ReaderService.com

YOUR READER'S SURVEY
"THANK YOU" FREE GIFTS INCLUDE:
- ▶ 2 FREE books
- ▶ 2 lovely surprise gifts

PLEASE FILL IN THE CIRCLES COMPLETELY TO RESPOND

1) What type of fiction books do you enjoy reading? (Check all that apply)
   ○ Suspense/Thrillers ○ Action/Adventure ○ Modern-day Romances
   ○ Historical Romance ○ Humor ○ Paranormal Romance

2) What attracted you most to the last fiction book you purchased on impulse?
   ○ The Title ○ The Cover ○ The Author ○ The Story

3) What is usually the greatest influencer when you <u>plan</u> to buy a book?
   ○ Advertising ○ Referral ○ Book Review

4) How often do you access the internet?
   ○ Daily ○ Weekly ○ Monthly ○ Rarely or never

5) How many NEW paperback fiction novels have you purchased in the past 3 months?
   ○ 0 - 2 ○ 3 - 6 ○ 7 or more

YES! I have completed the Reader's Survey. Please send me the 2 FREE books and 2 FREE gifts (gifts are worth about $10 retail) for which I qualify. I understand that I am under no obligation to purchase any books, as explained on the back of this card.

235/335 HDL GLN4

FIRST NAME	LAST NAME

ADDRESS

APT.#	CITY

STATE/PROV.	ZIP/POSTAL CODE

type of thing herself. "Aiyana's name is unusual. Is it Nicaraguan?"

"Consuelo claims it's Native American for eternal flower. A woman who was part Cherokee came to her rescue one night when she was so hungry and tired she was ready to collapse. German was crying. Neither one of them could go a step farther. So she hid in a barn, hoping to rest before pushing on—only to be discovered by this woman whose name was Aiyana. Consuelo thought she'd be reported or turned out, but Aiyana fed them dinner and gave them a bed to sleep in. To this day, Consuelo says Aiyana was an angel sent from God, that she wasn't really human."

"That's a beautiful story, too."

"Consuelo's lived a challenging but interesting life. Fortunately, other than old age, her worries are behind her. Hank takes care of her every need. Grandma Sway, as we called her growing up, is the one who gave me my horse," he added.

"Atsila?"

"Yeah. Apparently, the Aiyana who helped her had a horse by the same name, which she gave to Consuelo so that Consuelo would have some mode of transportation, and so that German wouldn't have to walk anymore. Without that horse, Consuelo swears she and German would not have survived the next two weeks. Not long after, she had to sell it, which broke her heart, but she claims she would've starved without that money."

"How kind. What does Atsila mean?"

"I don't know. I tried looking it up once but couldn't find anything definitive—other than that it has Native American roots." He came closer and took the picture from her to look more carefully at it himself. "I figure the real meaning doesn't matter, anyway. To me, it means compassion."

"I bet the original Aiyana would be proud of her name-sake," Cora said. "Your mother seems to be very generous herself."

"Yes. Not only has she helped me and my brothers, she's helped so many."

After what Eli had been subjected to, he'd deserved his own "angel." So did the others. And yet Cora couldn't help feeling rejected, jealous, left out, overlooked…*something* that felt like a knife to the heart. "Has she said why she's never had any biological children?"

"No. I've always assumed that maybe she couldn't."

Cora stood as living proof that Aiyana wasn't infertile. But, of course, she couldn't say anything to refute the assumption. "Darci told me that Cal Buchanon has been in love with her for years."

"They spend a lot of time together, more than she lets on to me or anyone else, if she can help it."

"She must care for him, too."

"I'm pretty sure she does."

"What gives?"

He scratched his neck. "She's afraid of getting hurt, or feels as if devoting herself to a relationship like that will take away from her work or something. I can't figure it out myself. And she won't talk about it." He put the picture back on the piano. "Why does this stuff seem to mean so much to *you*?"

Only then did Cora realize she was being too transparent. Straightening, she forced back the frustration and disappointment, as well as the curiosity she'd manifested so far, and conjured a polite expression. "I didn't mean to give you the impression it was overly important. I was curious, that's all."

Fortunately, he didn't get the chance to question her further. At that point, Aiyana called them to dinner.

Chapter Eleven

During the meal, Dallas tried to tease Cora about last night with a few carefully placed innuendos. But it seemed to Eli that Cora was too distracted and preoccupied to focus on Dallas or what he said, even when he made reference to what'd happened outside the bar. She'd smile or laugh where appropriate, but only Aiyana could claim her full attention. By the end of dinner, after Cora had helped Aiyana put the leftover pot roast, vegetables, mashed potatoes and cheesecake in the fridge and do the dishes, Eli was feeling a bit neglected. He got the distinct impression that she'd come to see his mother, that he had nothing to do with her desire to join them, especially when, instead of watching TV with everyone else, the two women went into the living room and talked for over an hour.

When he got up to fetch a glass of water, or he simply made an effort to listen, he could hear various bits and pieces of their conversation. Most of it was about the ranch—Aiyana's philosophy for the school, the fact that she'd chosen to place New Horizons in Silver Springs because it had wide-open spaces but wasn't too far from a major population center, why she'd adopted each one of her sons and which students she was concerned about this year.

He thought he might finally get a few crumbs of Cora's attention when they rejoined the group— even if it was only a quick, private smile. Instead, as soon as they finished visiting, Cora said she should go, that she had to get ready for her classes in the morning.

They'd made crazy, impromptu, almost animalistic love outside at the bar last night and then again in the shower this morning, but she'd hardly given him the time of day since coming to dinner.

"Thanks so much for having me," she told Aiyana. "You have a lovely home and a wonderful family."

"You're welcome. It's nice to have a little estrogen in the house," she said with a laugh. "You must join us again next Sunday. Dallas won't be here. He leaves on Tuesday. But Eli, Gavin, Liam and Bentley will."

"I'll do that, but only if you let me bring the dessert or another dish."

"I'm sure I could be persuaded," Aiyana told her.

"It was really great to meet you," Cora said to Dallas. "I'm sorry you have to leave town so soon."

"There are mountains to climb," he joked as he got up to hug her goodbye. Eli got off the couch, too, and was standing close enough to hear Dallas whisper something like, "Take good care of my brother."

Whether that was really what Dallas said or not, Cora turned and gave him a dutiful hug, one no different from the kind she'd imparted to everyone else. "Again, thank you."

"Eli, why don't you walk her out?" Aiyana piped up as Cora grabbed her purse.

Eli wasn't sure if that suggestion was as random as Aiyana pretended, but he didn't care. He was eager for a few minutes alone with Cora, so he was grateful his mother had tapped him instead of one of his brothers. "Sure."

"Dinner was wonderful," Cora said as they strolled down the drive side by side, without touching. "Now that my brother and I are adults, my mother doesn't bother to cook anymore. She's very generous about inviting us over for carryout, or taking us to a restaurant, so I'm not complaining. But a big Sunday meal from scratch? That's almost unheard of these days."

"It's not like it was a sacrifice to have you. You can come back next Sunday. You heard my mom."

"I'd like that," she said, but he didn't get the impression he was the reason she'd like it, and that bothered him.

"Are you really going home to get ready for classes?" he asked as he opened her car door for her.

"Yeah. I promised my students we'd start ceramics this week. Now that I'm more familiar with their skill level, I need to figure out the ideal project and how much time it will require on the throwing wheel."

He almost said, *And if I'd like to see you again?* but he got the distinct impression that something was causing her to distance herself from him and he'd be stupid to push.

"You look incredible in that dress," he said instead, which was the truth. Ever since she'd arrived, he'd had difficulty looking anywhere except at her.

He was glad he'd told her that when, at last, she focused on him—and smiled. "Thank you," she said, but she didn't try to set up their next meeting, didn't ask if he'd call, didn't say a word about getting together with him again. "Good night," she added, and that was his signal to close the door.

The TV played in the background as Cora curled up on her couch and thumbed through the file the private investigator had, after much searching, provided on Aiyana. There wasn't a great deal in it, just some basic background information—where and when Aiyana was born, where she grew up, a couple of articles on New Horizons. Thanks to California's adoption laws, Cora had been unable to get the records that were sealed by the court. She'd had an attorney working on that, but because of various details her adoptive mother had let slip—like where and when she was born and at which hospital—the private investigator had come through first. So she'd given up on pursuing the court order. Several states had unsealed their adoption records. She hoped California would soon follow suit. Then maybe she'd be able to find out who her father was—if his name was on her original birth certificate. Adoptees had access only to their ABC or Amended Birth Certificate, which not only facilitated the change in the name of the parents but could list a different place of birth. In some instances, agencies even altered the *day* of birth. Fortunately, Cora hadn't been given a new birthday. Otherwise, chances were she never would've found Aiyana.

Or…maybe that would've been for the best. She'd spoken to several other adoptees, online and otherwise, who'd told her to be careful what she wished for. They'd been disappointed in their birth mothers, but she was not. She respected Aiyana, admired her and wished she could be part of her life in a more significant way than merely working for her. But she couldn't see how she'd ever be able to do that if she was still sleeping with Elijah.

Regardless of Elijah, did she dare—or even have the right—to upset Aiyana's life by announcing her true identity? Would Aiyana be happy to have found her?

That would probably depend on the reason Aiyana had given her up, and there was no file, attorney or private detective who could provide that information. Perhaps her grandmother could shed some light on the matter, but even that wasn't guaranteed. It was possible Consuelo had never been made aware of the pregnancy. Aiyana had had Cora when she was twenty-one, so she'd been an adult but not a well-seasoned one. Maybe Consuelo hadn't approved of the relationship that'd left Aiyana pregnant, and that was part of the reason Aiyana had acted as she did.

After staring at the grainy picture in the newspaper clipping that'd given Cora her first glimpse of Aiyana, she put down the file and picked up her phone. She hadn't yet returned Lilly's call. She needed to do that, didn't want her adoptive mother to feel as if she was being neglected.

"There you are!" her mother exclaimed as soon as she answered. "How are you, sweetheart?"

Cora rubbed her left temple with her free hand. "I'm doing great. How are you, Mom?"

"Missing you. It's not the same without you here. I have no one to go shopping with," she said in a pouty voice that Cora knew was a joke.

"I'll go shopping with you when I visit next."

"Yes. We'll have you try on that dress I found. You're going to love it."

"I'm sure I will."

"Your father and I thought you might come home again this weekend, we're sad when we didn't see you. What'd you do?"

Cora considered mentioning that she'd had dinner at Aiyana's but decided it wasn't necessary. "I've met a new friend—another teacher here at the school named Darci. We went out last night."

"How nice. I'm so relieved you're adjusting. I was afraid you wouldn't like it, and this year would prove long and miserable. I was surprised when you decided to go there instead of accepting the position at Woodbridge. But you don't regret it?"

"No. Not at all," she said, and that was mostly true. If nothing else, the rabid curiosity that'd nearly driven her mad over the years had been appeased, to a point. As she finished talking to her mother she had to admit, however, that she had no idea if she'd regret what she was doing in the end.

Chapter Twelve

Cora knew she shouldn't have accepted when Eli texted her while she was at lunch the following day to see if he could take her horseback riding in the evening. After having dinner at Aiyana's, she was more aware than ever that she was putting them all in a difficult position. She'd decided to back away, had assumed she still had the fortitude—until she heard from him this afternoon and had thrown all of that out the window with a "one more time" excuse.

When he'd explained where to meet him, she'd guessed he was taking her to the same place he'd taken the boys—not that she intended to reveal the fact that she'd seen him here before. He'd been so carefree that day, so…unguarded. That memory was the one thing she planned to take away from this place when school let out—probably because she'd only seen Elijah like that once or twice since, when he was so caught up in their lovemaking that he dropped the aloof mask he wore otherwise. She felt like those moments were the only ones where she got to see the vulnerable heart beneath that rugged chest.

A silver truck towing a white trailer turned off the highway and parked in the clearing where she'd left her car. When she stepped out of the trees and greeted Eli, he responded with an uncharacteristically wide smile, one that suggested he was happy to see her, which made her glad she'd come. He usually kept his emotions more carefully concealed.

"Have you ever ridden before?" he asked as he pulled on a pair of leather gloves.

"Once. In Mexico. It was a four-hour-long trail ride with my family on the beach, and it was beautiful. But my horse was only allowed to walk slowly behind the horse in front."

"That's not really riding."

"After the first hour or so, it got boring," she admitted.

"You'll like this better."

She expected him to be towing two horses, but when he opened the trailer, she saw only Atsila. "We're riding together?"

"Is that okay? I figured if you're not familiar with horses, you might feel more comfortable riding double."

Since all she wanted to do was touch him—didn't care if they ever left the clearing—she had no reason to complain. "No problem."

"Great. I'll let you take the reins whenever."

He led the horse out and lifted Cora into the saddle before securing the truck and the trailer. Then he walked over and swung up behind her.

The warmth of his body made her wish she could turn and kiss him. They'd trained their bodies to expect such contact when they saw each other. She wasn't even sure what they were doing here. She liked the idea of riding, but it felt as if they were wasting what little time they could spend together.

They traveled mostly in silence. Cora got the impression Eli didn't care to talk. He'd answer if she asked a question, but only with a simple yes or no, if possible. There were a few minutes when she took the reins, but as soon as they came to a narrow pass that she wasn't confident in navigating, he took over.

"What made you ask me to go riding?" she asked as they continued to climb the mountain.

"You'll see," he replied, and that was it. Apparently, she was waiting for something. She didn't find out what until they crested the top of the mountain, where the trees thinned, revealing a stunning red-and-gold sunset.

"Wow," she murmured.

He pulled the horse to a stop. "Have you ever seen anything more beautiful?"

If she were being objective, some of the sunsets she'd seen at the beach and around the world were as spectacular. Cognitively, she knew that. But he'd brought her out here because he wanted her to enjoy this, and that made it the best darn sunset in the world. "Not with you," she said.

"What does that mean?"

"It means I'd like it even if it wasn't nearly so beautiful."

One hand came up to catch her chin as he finally kissed her. She wasn't entirely sure how everything went from there. Somehow, in a matter of minutes, they were off the horse and on the ground, their clothes open and askew, kissing and exploring and enjoying what they'd wanted from the first moment they met up.

"You can't be comfortable out here," he said with some regret, as if he hated to stop but felt too much guilt to continue. "I'll take you back down."

"No." Cora wasn't ready to leave. Not yet. When he pulled away to get up, she pressed him onto his back. Then she nibbled at his neck and his bare chest as she moved down—and heard him draw a sharp breath as she took him into her mouth.

They drove home separately, just as they'd come, as if they hadn't been together. Because Eli hadn't said anything about meeting up later, Cora assumed their ride—and what had occurred on it—was the end of their time with each other for today. She spent the next couple of hours getting ready for her classes tomorrow while trying to build up her resistance to him—so she wouldn't melt so quickly when he called or texted her the next time—only to have him surprise her by showing up at her door as she was getting ready for bed.

He didn't explain why he'd come; he didn't need to. He stepped inside as if he had every right and pulled her into his arms. Then it was like the ride earlier, when they couldn't pull each other's clothes off fast enough. She managed to remove his shirt and toss it aside before he kissed her again. Then he lifted her into his arms and she wrapped her legs around his narrow hips and let him carry her into the bedroom, where they fell onto her bed and made love.

On some level, Cora knew their affair was getting out of hand. They couldn't seem to stem the desire they felt for each other—the more he touched her, the more she craved his touch, and he seemed to be every bit as caught in the same web.

What happened to getting satisfied and moving on? she asked herself when it was all over and he was dozing beside her. That had been the original plan, but the opposite seemed to be taking place. Just watching him sleep made her feel so much tenderness it frightened her. She was losing her heart to a man who'd told her he wasn't to be trusted with it.

What am I going to do?

She reached over to push the hair off his forehead, and he opened his eyes. Since it was nearly eleven, she thought he'd get up and leave. They both had to work in the morning. Instead, he drew her into the curve of his body and, after a kiss on her bare shoulder, drifted off again.

Apparently, he didn't feel any pressure to get home at a reasonable hour. Or he was enjoying being with her too much to put an end to it. She preferred to believe the latter, but feared she was building things up in her head—a dangerous practice in its own right.

She wondered where he'd parked his truck, and guessed

that he'd left it at home and walked over. He wasn't stupid, wouldn't be that obvious.

Slowly, she allowed herself to succumb to the comfort and satisfaction of having him there next to her. She was going to be hurt; she had little doubt about that. But it wasn't going to be tonight. She'd merely take their relationship moment by moment, she decided—and the next thing she knew, her alarm was going off the following morning, and Eli was still in her bed.

Since he hadn't reacted to the alarm, she reached over to touch his shoulder. He needed to get out of the house before everyone on campus was up and moving around. But before she could even touch him, someone knocked on the front door.

That brought his head up immediately. "Doug?" he said without preamble.

She bit her lip. "It's only seven. I can't imagine he'd pop over so early."

He scrubbed a hand over his face. "Maybe he has more vegetables."

"He hasn't brought any since the last time. He's been much better about leaving me alone," she said as she got up and hurried to don a robe. She had to answer the door. Whoever it was would know she was home. Her car was in the drive. "Your mother must've spoken to him even though she told me she wouldn't."

"*She* didn't speak to him—*I* did," he said.

She paused to gawk at him. "What did you say?"

"Nothing. I just told him to keep his distance."

She laughed. Of course it would be that simple for him. No glossing over anything, no mincing words. Just the bottom line: *stop*.

"What's so funny?" he asked.

"Nothing." She pulled the belt of her robe tight. "My hair's not *too* crazy, is it?"

He grinned.

"That must be a no."

Whoever was at the door knocked again, causing her to glance toward the living room.

"You look like you've had a busy night," he said, that grin slanting to one side, "but I wouldn't want to make you self-conscious."

"Thanks for doing just that," she whispered in mock outrage but couldn't help betraying herself with a smile of her own. Maybe he wasn't capable of trusting her enough to give her his heart, but he was incredibly good in bed, especially now that they were becoming more comfortable with each other. She also liked these little moments when he revealed that he *did* have a playful side.

"It's a great look on you," he said.

She didn't take the time to answer. "Stay here. And don't make any noise," she said as she left the bedroom.

Once she reached the door, she tried to smooth her hair down one final time as she peered through the peep hole.

It wasn't Doug; it was Aiyana. Cora wanted to alert Eli to the fact that his mother was standing on the stoop, but she'd delayed too long already and couldn't call back for fear Aiyana would hear her through the panel.

Cora could only hope she hadn't come here looking for her son... "Hi," she said as she opened the door.

Aiyana's lips curved into a pleasant smile. "I'm sorry to bother you so early."

"It's no trouble," she said but couldn't help wondering why this couldn't have waited until she was in her classroom. "I was rolling out of bed, anyway."

"I figured you'd be up, what with school starting in little over an hour. There's a guy who looks like he's had a pretty rough night at the administration building, asking for you. I tried to reach you on your cell but couldn't get an answer. Apparently, he's been trying to reach you, too."

She hadn't taken her cell out of her purse last night to charge it. "The battery must be dead. Did this man say who he is?"

"He said you broke up with him when you left LA."

Matt? *Damn...* "I—I'll... Sorry about the random visit. Let me get showered and I'll be right over."

"Would you rather I send him here?"

It was going to be hard enough for Eli to get out of her house without being seen. "No. Um...have him wait there. I'll come as soon as I can."

"Okay." Her gaze shifted to something behind Cora. "Tell my son I said good morning," she added and left.

Cora pivoted to discover Elijah's shirt on the floor. Shoot! Now there would be no pretending that she and Eli were only friends.

Eli came to the doorway, wearing nothing. "What'd she say?"

Cora picked up his shirt and handed it to him. "She said to tell you hello."

To Cora's surprise, he didn't seem to be upset by that. He scratched his head and said, "I mean before that."

"My ex-boyfriend is at the office." Looking like he'd been up all night. *Why?* Cora hadn't spoken to him since moving to Silver Springs.

"What does he want?"

"I have no idea," she replied but realized her phone might provide the answer. She plugged it in and waited for it to charge while Eli dressed. She was just listening to the many messages Matt had left when Eli walked out of the bedroom again.

"You're not coming back to me? I thought we loved each other. But you must never have cared for me the way I cared for you."

Instead of heading to the door, Eli walked over to the counter and listened to Matt's next message along with her.

"You're not going to answer your phone? Seriously? I can hardly breathe now that you're gone. Whatever I did wrong, I'll fix it, okay? I'll change. Just…give me another chance."

Cora clicked away from her voice mail. She figured Eli had heard enough.

"He wants you back," he said.

"Apparently."

He raked his fingers through his hair. "How do *you* feel?"

"I feel bad that I've hurt him."

She knew that wasn't the answer Eli had been looking for, but she didn't care to address anything else. She had to shower, hurry over to see what she could do for Matt and get to class—all before eight thirty.

"You're upset he's here."

"I'm upset that your mother knows about us."

"Because…"

Because Aiyana was her birth mother, and now, if she ever decided to have that conversation, it would be even harder. She was ruining any hope she had of reuniting with Aiyana as the daughter she was! But she hadn't planned on Aiyana having an adopted son she couldn't resist. "I respect her. I don't want her to think poorly of me."

"She doesn't think poorly of you. She likes you."

For some reason, that simple statement nearly made Cora burst into tears. He'd spoken so casually, as if he was saying, "Why would you matter much to her either way?"

Aiyana was her *mother*. She wanted more than the courteous treatment other teachers received.

When she started to blink fast, trying to hold back the tears, he walked over and rested his hands on her shoulders. "I'm sorry I stayed over. If you'll still see me in the future, I'll be more careful."

"I'm not blaming you. This has nothing to do with

you." She could've asked him to go at any moment, but she hadn't—because she'd wanted him to stay right where he was. Her emotional reaction to Aiyana's appearance was about something else, something he couldn't even begin to guess because he, most likely, didn't know his mother had ever had a child of her own.

"Then it's your ex that has you upset."

She dashed a hand across her cheek. "Matt? No. It's nothing."

She could tell he wasn't sure what to say next. "I'm fine," she added.

"I'm sorry," he said again, as if he hated to see her like this, especially because he suspected he might be part of the cause.

"It's nothing, like I said."

"Okay." He had to get to school, too, and she knew it. Although he acted reluctant to walk away at this juncture, he seemed to understand there was nothing more he could do. After pressing a kiss to her forehead, he left.

Chapter Thirteen

The day seemed to last forever. Knowing that Matt was sleeping at her house, waiting for her to get out of school, made Cora glance at the clock—and grind her teeth—over and over. Time seemed to be standing still. She didn't want her ex-boyfriend in Silver Springs, couldn't believe he'd come down here.

As soon as the lunch bell sounded and the students filed out of her classroom, she considered going home. She had thirty minutes or so she could use to talk to Matt. But she preferred to wait until she could sit down with him at length and hash out whatever he felt he needed to go over. Then maybe she could send him on his way knowing that was the end, once and for all.

While she was standing at the window, watching the students who'd already finished their lunch mill about campus, Eli walked in.

"Hey."

She turned and straightened. He'd never come to her room before. "Hi."

"I didn't see you in the cafeteria so…I thought I'd bring you some lunch." He lifted a brown sack.

She'd eaten an apple from her desk drawer. She hadn't had it in her to face him or Aiyana, in case either one of them happened to be in the cafeteria. "I've had too much to do here."

The fact that she'd been staring outside, doing nothing, contradicted that statement, but he didn't point it out. He carried her lunch over to the desk. "You feeling okay?"

"Yeah."

"What happened with Matt?"

"Nothing. Yet. I had to get to my first class, and he looked like he wasn't feeling great, so I told him to sleep until I get out of school."

He rubbed a hand over his smooth-shaven chin. "You'll talk to him when you get home."

"Yes." She peered into the sack to find a turkey sandwich, some celery and carrot sticks and a big chocolate chip cookie. "This is very nice of you. Thank you."

"No problem."

He didn't seem to be in any hurry to leave.

"Did your mother say anything to you about this morning?" she asked as she broke off part of the cookie.

"We've been too busy."

"*Will* she say something?"

"I doubt it. For the most part, she's pretty good about minding her own business."

Cora wondered about his biological mother. Did he ever hear from her? Did he care about her—*could* he care? "Aiyana seems really great."

"She is." He checked his watch. "I've got to go."

"Thanks for stopping by."

He hesitated at the door. "Will you call me when Matt's gone?"

"I don't know," she admitted.

"Nothing's changed, Cora," he said.

What was he talking about? *Everything* had changed. She was falling in love with him, which was exactly what he'd warned her not to do. And Matt knew about Aiyana! If she didn't handle him carefully enough, he could tell everyone what she was *really* doing in Silver Springs. "There have to be other girls you can…be with. You might have to drive to LA once in a while, but someone like you… you'd have no problem getting laid."

He winced as if she'd slapped her. "I never said the

person I was with didn't matter—that it could be anyone. And I hope I haven't treated you that way."

He hadn't. He'd been a dream lover—as considerate and kind as she could ever expect him to be. He'd also been clear about his limitations. Despite all her big talk, *she* was the one who couldn't seem to live up to their agreement.

She opened her mouth to apologize, but it was too late. He was gone.

Cora's stomach was twisted into knots by the time school let out and she was able to hurry home. Part of her wished Matt would simply be gone—that once he'd sobered up he'd been embarrassed and eager to get out of Silver Springs. She'd said everything she wanted to say to him when they broke up. And, because of him, she felt as if she'd somehow hurt, frustrated or disappointed Eli.

But Matt wasn't gone. He called out to her from the bedroom the moment he heard her come through the door.

Since she had such a small place, and only one bed, he was in it. After having shared that same bed with Eli only the night before, seeing Matt there felt so strange. But she hadn't invited Matt to New Horizons. She was merely being kind—and cautious—by giving him a place to rest until they could discuss whatever he'd come here to discuss.

"How was school?" He propped himself up with her pillows as she walked into the room and put her purse on the dresser.

That he was just rousing indicated he'd slept since she'd been gone, which answered *that* question. She hadn't missed an opportunity to get rid of him. "Today? Tedious."

"You don't like teaching here?"

She sat on the edge of the bed. "Normally, I do. But I was on pins and needles knowing you were waiting for me. What's going on?"

"What do you mean?"

"Why did you drive down here? Show up unexpectedly—and at least partially intoxicated? You could've killed yourself or someone else, driving that way."

"I wasn't drunk!"

She suspected he'd started out that way. He was lucky he hadn't had an accident, and that he hadn't been picked up. "You were disheveled and smelling of alcohol."

"Because my mother was just diagnosed with Alzheimer's, Cora. If you'd been staying in touch at all, you'd know that."

Cora clasped her hands together. "I'm sorry. I know that you were afraid…that you suspected something was wrong, but…"

"One day last week, she forgot we broke up. Asked when you were going to come see her."

"I'm sorry," she said again. She felt terrible about what was happening to Matt's mother. Sara was a lovely woman, certainly didn't deserve something like this. But there was nothing Cora could do about his mother's condition, wasn't sure what he expected. "I'll stop by to see her next time I'm in town."

"Next time you're in town," he echoed. "You say that as if you don't really care about her."

"Of course I care. I've always liked your mother."

"Well, she *loved* you. She thought you'd become her daughter-in-law, would've offered you all the love you feel as if you've had to live without, being adopted."

"It's not that I feel as if I haven't been loved, Matt. You don't understand at all, if that's what you think. I appreciate my parents—"

"Then why are you here instead of in LA with us?" he broke in. "Can't you tell how much I'm struggling without you? You haven't called me, haven't texted me. You haven't responded to anything I've posted on social media."

She hadn't viewed his social media, had quit doing that sort of thing even before she started seeing Eli.

"I thought you'd be back once you realized we had a good thing," he went on. "There's nothing better out there, you know."

In ways, what she had with Eli was better. They didn't have a label for what they were to each other, had no commitment, but she'd never felt so love drunk in her life than when she saw him or felt his hands on her body. "I've been moving, starting a new job. That takes focus," she responded lamely.

"It can't take up every minute. You don't even know anyone down here. Aren't you lonely?"

"I've made a few friends."

"So you've kissed all your old friends goodbye."

She got up. "Not at all. I'm staying in touch. But we weren't *friends*, Matt. We were more than friends, and now we're broken up. Why would I confuse you or…or give you any reason to hope by remaining in contact? Maybe later, in a few years, when we've both had a chance to move on, we can reconnect. But it's too soon right now."

He shoved himself into a sitting position. "What are you saying?"

She threw up her hands. "What I told you before. I'm really sorry, especially about your mother. I don't want her to suffer. I don't want you to suffer, either. But I can't reciprocate what you're feeling. I don't know a nicer way of putting it, except to be honest. You're a wonderful guy, and I'll always care about you, but—"

"Who's going to treat you better?" he interrupted, his eyes snapping with challenge.

"No one! I have no complaints about the way you treated me. I said you were a great guy—"

"But you think your birth mother is somehow going to make your life better."

"Meeting Aiyana has already answered so many of

my questions," she said. "The curiosity I felt was half the problem."

When he got out of bed, she was relieved to see that he was still wearing all his clothes. "So you're glad you did it."

That would depend on what happened from here. She had to admit that things weren't looking good, not with a one-sided relationship developing between her and Eli and Aiyana showing up to find his shirt on her floor. But she couldn't say she regretted coming to Silver Springs, because she didn't. She was glad she'd met Aiyana, glad she knew where she came from and what her birth mother was like. She was also glad she'd met Eli. Otherwise, she might never have experienced the kind of passion he could evoke. Everyone deserved to encounter that magical feeling at least once in a lifetime. The fact that she hadn't been more passionate about Matt only confirmed that she'd been right to break things off with him. "I did what I needed to do."

"That doesn't answer the question."

"Then, yes, I'm glad."

His face fell. "You don't care about me anymore."

Not in the way he wanted her to. Hadn't she said that—many times? "I'd like to be friends—when you're ready," she reiterated.

Dropping his head, he rubbed his temples. "You're making a mistake, Cora. We are meant to be together."

She let her breath go in a sigh. "I can't change how I feel."

He folded his arms as he studied her. "Fine. Then…can I just ask for one last favor?"

"Of course."

"Let me stay here a few days? I need some time away from LA—to get my head around this and come to terms with my mother's diagnosis."

"I don't see how that will help."

"I'm telling you I can't go back. Not yet. You say you

care about me. Let me hang out for a while, talk things through."

She didn't want him to stay. As far as she was concerned, he couldn't hit the highway fast enough. But she did feel terrible about his mother's diagnosis. And she thought having Matt around might finally stop her from seeing Eli. So there was that, too. If Matt got his way, at least in that regard, maybe he'd believe she really *did* wish him well and would leave peaceably, without saying anything that would give her away to Aiyana or anyone else.

"I have only this one bed," she said. "You'll have to sleep on the couch. You realize that. I won't get physical with you. There's not even a remote chance."

"Fine. I understand. I'm happy just to be able to spend some time with you to sort of…grow accustomed to our new roles. I mean…if you're sincere about being friends."

"Of course I'm sincere!"

"What happened before was too abrupt."

"I got that. You can stay until Friday," she said. "But I doubt you'll really care to hang out that long. I'll be at work most of the time, and you'll be sitting around here alone, bored stiff."

"At least we can spend our evenings together. Let me stay until Saturday, though, okay? My aunt's in town to visit my mom, and I don't really want to see her. You know we butt heads. Being out of town gives me a good excuse to avoid another argument with the old curmudgeon."

"So long as it's Saturday *morning*," she said. And she hoped it would be early, before the day could really begin, so she'd have the rest of the weekend to herself. She was already looking forward to that.

"Okay," he said.

She forced herself to return his smile. She supposed, after two years together, she could give him that much. What was three or four days?

* * *

"What's wrong?"

Eli blinked and then focused on his brother Gavin. They were sitting at the bar on Friday, listening to the music and watching the people who were dancing—had gone out at his request because he'd needed the distraction. The football team had a bye this week, so he didn't even have that to think about this weekend. "Nothing, why?"

"You're not the same tonight."

He took a sip of his beer. "I don't know what you're talking about."

"You're preoccupied, quiet."

Because he couldn't help remembering what'd happened here the last time. "I'm tired."

The waitress stopped to gather Gavin's empty bottle and to see if she could get him another beer. "No, thanks," he told her. "So how's Cora?" he asked as she walked off. "Everything going okay with her?"

It wasn't going at all. Eli hadn't heard from her since he delivered her lunch on Tuesday. He'd looked for her in the cafeteria and on campus since, but if he happened to find her and catch her eye, she'd look away and leave the area soon after.

He kept telling himself he didn't care. That she'd decided to quit seeing him, which saved him from having to break things off later. Every romantic relationship he had came down to that eventually...

But this was different. She'd quit on him long before he was ready to let her go. The thought of her in that small house with her ex-boyfriend made him sick inside. He kept going over and over their time together, remembering the way she'd smile when he came toward her, the way she'd laugh if he said something funny, the way she made love without coming off so needy that she wound up making him feel cornered and desperate to get away.

And then he'd wonder what more he could've done to make her want to continue seeing him. "I guess. She's been busy."

"Meaning...what? You haven't seen her?"

He gripped his bottle that much tighter as a vision of her pressed up against the back of this very building filled his head. "Not recently."

"But you guys were so hot for each other when we were here last. I had to dance with Darci half a dozen songs in a row to keep her occupied."

Eli mustered a faint smile for Gavin's sacrifice, hoping that would finally put an end to the conversation. But Gavin went right back after it.

"Does that mean it's over?"

"Do we *have* to talk about this?" he finally snapped.

"Whoa! Okay. I see how it is."

Irritated that Gavin would even bring her up, Eli threw a few bucks on the table and stood. "Let's go. I should never have suggested we come here."

"God, you've been a bear the past couple of days," Gavin complained. "I've never seen you in such a sour mood. I'm not trying to piss you off, big brother—I'm just trying to figure out what's wrong. So cut me some slack!"

"Nothing's wrong. I don't know how many times I have to say..." The door opened, and he let his words trail away as Cora walked in with a tall, thin guy who had long, curly brown hair, a goatee and glasses. He would've finished his statement, but he could no longer remember what he'd been about to say.

This was Matt. Eli had known he was still in town. He'd walked over to Cora's a time or two and spotted the additional car in her drive.

Gavin followed his gaze. "Shit. She's with someone else now? *Who is that guy?*"

Eli couldn't make himself look away. "Her ex-boyfriend's in town."

"They're back together?"

He didn't know what the situation was. She hadn't told him, and he hadn't approached her to ask. He'd been trying to give her the space she seemed to want, had been hoping that by not pressuring her, she'd miss him the way he was missing her and come around again. "I guess."

"Ah! Finally, it all makes sense!"

"What makes sense?" Eli growled.

"You really liked her."

He said nothing.

"I've never known a woman to get under your skin before, but she's managed to do that, hasn't she?"

"You don't know anything," he grumbled.

Cora couldn't have seen his truck outside, because Gavin drove. Eli was waiting for her to realize he was there—and watched her nearly trip over her own feet the moment her eyes landed on him. She hesitated for a moment. Then she said something to Matt and they changed direction, walking around the perimeter of the bar to the other side.

"You okay?" Gavin asked while Cora and Matt found a table.

"Yeah. Sure." Eli tossed back what was left in his bottle. "Let's get out of here," he said, but he received a text while Gavin drove them home that only made his night worse.

"That her?" Gavin asked when Eli pulled out his phone to look at it. "Cora, I mean?"

Eli felt his stomach knot as he stared at the message. "No." He wished it was Cora. Maybe he wouldn't feel quite so terrible if she'd asked him to come back to the bar, or requested a few moments to talk.

Gavin gave him a funny look. "So…is it Mom?"

Not the mother Gavin meant and not the mother Eli

claimed. But that was the name by which she called herself. "It's nobody," he said. Nobody to *him*, anyway.

Determined to ignore this message like those that had come before, he slid his phone back into his pocket.

Chapter Fourteen

"Who was that guy?" Matt asked as Eli and Gavin headed for the door.

Cora's cheeks ached from clenching her jaw. She preferred to ignore that question, but she had to say *something*. The way Eli had stared them down as they came in had made an impression on Matt. She should never have brought him here. She wouldn't have, if she'd had any clue that Elijah would be here, too. She'd just been looking for some way to entertain him, to help the time pass until he left tomorrow.

"Cora?" Matt pressed when she didn't answer.

"My boss," she replied.

"He didn't look happy."

For good reason. Eli had to be wondering if she'd taken her ex-boyfriend back. She planned to talk to him; she just couldn't do it while Matt was in town. She wanted to make sure their paths never crossed.

"What do you think's wrong with him?" he asked.

"He's under a lot of pressure," she replied.

"But if you work for him, why didn't he say hello?"

"I doubt he even saw us."

"*What?* He was staring at us the whole time we were trying to find a table."

Desperate to escape this conversation, Cora came to her feet. "I like this song. Let's dance."

They danced a lot, and Matt drank a lot, which distracted him enough that he didn't ask anything else about Eli. He seemed to be having fun, but Cora was just biding her time, couldn't wait for this interminable night to end. She kept him at the bar until she thought everyone at the ranch would be settled in for the night. Then she drove him back to her place.

"What time will you be heading out in the morning?" she asked as she turned off the highway onto the narrow road that led, after another two miles, to the school.

"Tomorrow?" He acted as if this was the first he'd heard of his going.

She gripped the steering wheel that much tighter as they rolled under the high arch at the front entrance. "Yeah. I said I'd let you stay until Saturday morning."

"But you've had to work the whole time. Why don't I leave on Sunday? That way, we can do something fun tomorrow."

"Matt, you said you needed some time to pull yourself together, and I've given you that. I've even let you stay long enough to avoid your difficult aunt."

"And I appreciate it. But what's the rush?" he asked. "We've been having a great time, haven't we?"

No. She couldn't take another day. "I'm done," she blurted.

"What does that mean?"

"I'm ready for you to go home."

She was afraid this would provoke a fight, but she'd run out of patience. He thought *he* was having a difficult time; well, she was having a hard time, too. She'd felt nauseous ever since she'd seen the look on Eli's face at the bar.

Matt opened his mouth to reply but she let out an involuntary gasp that silenced him.

Eli's truck was parked in front of her house.

Eli couldn't believe he was doing this. He'd never felt the need to chase after a woman, but Cora was driving him crazy.

Matt got out of the car when she did and came around by the trunk. Eli noticed his surprised expression but refused to let the fact that Matt was there get in the way. He strode over to Cora. "Can we talk?"

He'd taken her off guard; he could tell. She paused for several seconds as if searching for the best way to respond before she said, "Um…tomorrow, okay? Tomorrow would be better for me."

She didn't understand that he was desperate or he wouldn't be here. "I don't want to wait." He needed her, needed…something with the power to divert his thoughts and ease the rage burning like acid inside him. His biological mother had been texting and calling him relentlessly since he'd left the bar, saying she was in a bad way and needed his help. But she was a psychopath and a drug addict, so she was always in a bad way. He wasn't going to let her back into his life. He wasn't the person to call even if she had straightened up, not after all the cruelty he'd suffered at her hands.

He'd finally left his phone at his place and gone out for a drive, traveled aimlessly around the valley for two hours before making the decision to allow himself to go to Cora's. He had to resolve at least *one* thing that was bothering him. Otherwise, it felt like his head would explode. Although his birth mother had contacted him once or twice before, she'd never been quite so insistent.

You know it was that damn Tim I married who treated you so bad. Wasn't me. I wasn't involved in any of that.

She'd had the nerve to send such a text—a blatant lie—as if he hadn't been fully aware of exactly what happened, and who was responsible. They'd been in it together, one feeding off the other. But it wasn't just that. He wasn't himself, wasn't in control, not since seeing Cora at the bar.

"This isn't… I mean, you're her boss," Matt said. "This isn't personal, right?"

Eli ignored him. He was wound up, on edge, afraid he'd

bash him in the face if he so much as acknowledged his presence. His birth mother triggered too many painful memories, a surfeit of emotion. Eli felt like there was a monster growing inside him that was about to bust out at any moment.

Fortunately, since Aiyana had taken him in and he'd worked through most of his issues—the ones he *could* resolve—he hadn't allowed his frustration to erupt, hadn't let it get the better of him.

But it'd been a long time since he'd been this raw.

"I asked you a question," Matt said.

Eli leveled a glare at him. "If you know what's good for you, you'll go inside."

Eyes wide, Matt stumbled back as if he'd just caught a glimpse of the rage lurking inside Eli, but before he could do anything else, Cora grabbed his arm and pulled him toward the house. "Give us a few minutes. Will you? Please?"

Unwilling to make it that easy, Matt looked from her to Eli and back again. "Don't tell me... You guys are seeing each other, aren't you!" He glared at her as if she'd cheated on him. "There's no way you'd start dating Aiyana's son! Not without—"

"Matt, if you say another word I'll never forgive you!" she broke in.

Without what? Eli had no clue and didn't get the chance to ask before she shoved her ex toward the house with more force. "Matt, please. If you value our friendship *at all*, you'll go inside this minute."

He cursed but accepted the keys she tossed him and finally did as she asked.

Once he was gone, a profound silence fell.

Suddenly, Eli was no longer sure what he'd hoped to achieve. His eyes were beginning to burn as badly as his gut, and a lump the size of a baseball rose in his throat, making it impossible for him to speak normally.

What the heck was he doing? He'd been a fool to come here. He was only making matters worse.

Without another word, he turned on his heel and opened his truck door. He intended to get in and drive off before she could realize how close he was to breaking down, but she grabbed hold of him.

"What is it, Eli?" She looked concerned as she dragged him around to face her, but that only made it harder for him to maintain his composure. He jerked away, didn't want her to see him like this. But she refused to let him go. She caught hold of him again, this time with a stronger grasp. "*Talk* to me!"

"It's okay. I'm sorry. I shouldn't have come here." He managed to mutter that much without having his voice crack—thank God—but she didn't act like she heard him. She stared into his face, trying to read what he was feeling. Then she wrapped her arms around his waist and pressed her cheek against his chest. "What is it?" she asked, clinging tightly. "Tell me."

He lifted his hands to her shoulders. He intended to push her away, couldn't believe he'd allowed himself to need her. He should've gone home like he was about to do now. He couldn't rely on her, on anyone, no matter how tempting it was to believe otherwise. But she wouldn't let go—and the next thing he knew his arms slid around her, securing her against him instead of breaking off the embrace.

"It's okay," she said.

He knew she could probably feel how badly he was shaking, but there was nothing he could do about that now. "Where've you been?" he asked.

Her hands slipped up the back of his shirt, and he felt her press her palms against his bare skin—a move he found both satisfying and intimate. She wasn't merely offering him a light "you'll be okay" pat. She was making it clear that she cared about him and wouldn't let him down. "It doesn't matter. I'm here now."

Burying his face in her hair, he gripped her that much tighter, and they stood like that until he could overcome all the terrible feelings that had him so twisted up inside. "Come home with me," he said at length, his mouth at her ear.

When she hesitated, he feared she'd refuse. She had Matt in the house, after all. He was asking a lot for her to leave her guest, but he needed to hear her say yes, needed to know that *he* came before Matt.

And, in the end, she murmured, "Okay."

Cora promised herself she'd tell Eli. Tonight. She had to. She didn't see how she could continue sleeping in his bed without divulging her connection to Aiyana. But, despite what he'd indicated at her place, Eli wasn't interested in having a discussion. That she'd go home with him was all that seemed important at the moment.

On the drive over, when she asked him what was wrong, he said he didn't want to talk about it. So she let the conversation lapse, but the ensuing silence wasn't awkward or upsetting. It was more like everything that'd been so wrong was now right, just because they were together.

The moment they reached his house, he tugged her inside and, without so much as turning on the light, began to let her know how badly he'd missed her. He wasn't *un*willing to communicate, she realized. He just preferred to speak to her in a different way, one in which he felt more capable of expressing himself.

She did get four words out of him—"I'm glad you're back." But that was all, and she wasn't willing to push. Something significant was going on between them that he didn't seem capable of putting into words, and she didn't need him to. She could feel the difference in the way he touched her.

His thick eyelashes rested on his cheeks as he ran his

tongue across her lips. "*You're* what I need," he said, surprising her by speaking again.

What'd happened tonight? He'd been so upset at her house he'd been trembling when she slid her arms around his waist. Just the memory of it made her defensive of him. She knew simply seeing her with Matt wasn't enough to cause a reaction like that. So what was it?

Regardless, she could feel that he was doing much better. His fingers curled and locked through hers as he bent his head to kiss her.

"You can kiss like no one else," she told him, relaxing as the desire he so easily evoked began to rise inside her once again.

"It's not difficult to kiss good when the person you're kissing tastes like honey," he told her and pulled back to look at her, seemingly content just to have her back in his house.

Cora might've been embarrassed to be the subject of such close scrutiny. She couldn't hide how deeply he affected her, so there was a certain vulnerability that came with holding his gaze. The fact that she did hold it, however—that she let him see she wasn't unaffected—appeared to be what he was looking for. His lips curved into a rather boyish smile and he kissed her again, even more softly, before leading her into his bedroom.

"Will you undress for me?" he asked as he sat on the bed.

Cora was tempted to derail that request by closing the gap between them. There'd be so much less risk in what they were doing if she could accelerate their lovemaking to the point that neither one of them was thinking clearly. Doing it with such *intention*—it almost felt like this was the first time they'd ever been together.

In a way it was, she realized. He was taking her more seriously, investing more time, effort and emotion. But… dared she take this step? *Before* telling him who she was?

"Relax. It's just me." He wanted her to trust him, to act

confidently, but by not telling him who she was, she was sort of lying to him...

Although she hesitated, in the end she couldn't bring herself to ruin this moment. She'd slept with Matt for two years and never experienced what it was like to make love in such a cerebral fashion, one in which her heart and mind were as active and involved as her body. Now she understood how many times she'd merely gone through the motions, either for her own physical release or simply to be a good partner and satisfy Matt.

Eli was much deeper than the women he'd been with had given him credit for, she decided. He had a tender heart; he merely protected it well. That he would reveal his sensitive side was making her fall that much harder.

Slowly, she removed her clothes.

"Gorgeous," he said, his expression rapt. "It's been *such* a long week."

His nostrils flared as she stepped closer. "At least it's going to end well," she said and guided his head to her breast, stroking his cheek as he suckled her.

His hands slid to her waist, then moved over her hips and around to the back, at which point he lifted her easily onto the bed before removing his own clothes.

"Do we need a condom?" he asked.

She'd been on the pill for a week. "According to what I've read online, we should be safe."

His teeth flashed in another smile. "I get to come inside you," he said and, when they both reached that pinnacle, Cora couldn't help but acknowledge that she'd never enjoyed making love to anyone more.

After an experience like that she wasn't willing to have the talk they needed to have about Aiyana. That would ruin everything, destroy the memory. So she promised herself she'd tell him in the morning and faded off to sleep, her arms and legs entwined with his.

Chapter Fifteen

"What are you going to do about Matt?"

Cora pulled herself out of the last vestiges of sleep so that she could answer Eli's question. He'd begun to stir several minutes ago, but she'd been reluctant to reach full consciousness, knew she'd have to face all that awaited her when she did. "I hope he got up and left," she mumbled. "He was supposed to leave this morning."

"What's he been doing here?"

She heard the caution in Eli's tone, could tell he was prepared for an answer he didn't like. "Sleeping on the couch."

"You didn't get back together with him."

"No."

He seemed so relieved when he reached for her that she smoothed her hand over his bare chest in a comforting fashion as she rested her head on his shoulder.

"What did he want, then?" he asked.

"He wanted to reconcile, but I wasn't interested."

"So why didn't he leave?"

"He asked if he could stay—to show me what I was missing, I suppose."

Eli lifted his head. "And you let him?"

"It's complicated."

"I can't imagine it would be that complicated to me."

Because he didn't know everything. She'd let Matt stay mostly to appease him. She'd been trying to end their relationship in such a way that he wouldn't cause trouble. With what he and his mother were going through, she'd also wanted to be supportive and prove she was sincere about maintaining a friendship. "We were together for two years. He said he was having a hard time getting over me, so I figured I owed him a few days to come to terms with our new relationship."

"Wouldn't being around you only make getting over the breakup harder?"

"I told him that. He argued that he needed to get used to our new status, and I thought it might give him the closure he seemed to be missing if I didn't rush him out the door."

"He didn't know about me."

That had been apparent in Matt's reaction last night. "Of course not. I haven't told anyone."

He dropped his head back. "Even your family at home?"

She understood what that would likely indicate to him— that she wasn't taking the relationship seriously. But she wasn't supposed to be taking the relationship seriously. "No. Why would I? You told me not to expect anything."

"You've certainly taken that to heart," he said wryly.

"I don't want to get hurt any more than you do."

"And now?"

"Has that changed?"

His fingers slipped through her hair. "You can't tell?"

She could tell last night. But there were still a lot of blanks to be filled in. She leaned up on her elbow to be able to see into his face. "What is it you want from me, Eli?" she asked. "Specifically."

He thought for a moment. Then he said, "I want to be with you while you're here."

"And what would that entail? A night together every once in a while?"

"I'm asking for a little more than that."

"But more equals…what? Would we quit trying to hide the fact that we're seeing each other?"

He sat up against the headboard. "Why not? That hasn't been the best-kept secret in the first place."

She pulled the sheet with her as she came into a sitting position, too. "What about dating other people?"

"We won't date other people." He spoke quickly enough to suggest he knew his mind on that matter without even having to think.

"We'd be exclusive."

"Yes, and we'll see each other a lot. Okay?" He lifted a hand to run a thumb down her jawline. "This past week just about killed me."

She assumed he was joking, so she chuckled, but he didn't laugh with her. He seemed serious. "You mean that," she said, sobering.

"I hated every minute of it."

"So...we'll be exclusive and see each other a lot—and then?"

"We'll deal with that when the time comes."

"No promises."

His eyebrows came together. "I told you I'm not good at this. I'm hoping I'll get better at it. But, either way, it's too early to try and decide what might come later."

He had a point. But she had a secret. Now that they had an understanding of sorts, would she be a fool to divulge that? What if she shared the circumstances surrounding her birth and he insisted she tell Aiyana? The deception could make Aiyana angry. Or there could be some reason Aiyana wouldn't or couldn't be around her. In that case, she'd lose her job, which wouldn't be the best thing for her or the school, not midyear. She liked it here, liked being with Elijah.

So, once again, she ignored her better judgment—put what she felt now above what she'd probably be feeling at the end of the school year—and decided to wait.

Fortunately, that was made easy when Eli's phone began to buzz, drawing their attention. He was getting a call or text. When he reached over to grab it, she thought he'd answer. But after checking the display, he cursed and tossed the phone back on the nightstand as if it had burned his hand.

"Who is it?" she asked.

Closing his eyes, he leaned his head against the wall again.

"Eli?" Whoever it was, he didn't like them—or wasn't happy they were trying to reach him. "It's not Aiyana…"

"No."

Of course not. Cora couldn't imagine he'd be unhappy to hear from one of his brothers, either. So…maybe it was an old girlfriend.

When she said nothing more, he opened his eyes and looked at her.

"What?" she said.

Instead of answering, he reclaimed his phone and showed her the text he'd received—How can you be so selfish? I only need $50.

She noted the name associated with that text. "*Maleficent's* texting you?"

"Jo Seifert. My mother."

"Maleficent's a Disney character, right? From *Sleeping Beauty?*"

"An evil character. Maleficent means doing harm."

His mother. She was tempted to touch the scar on his chin—she still didn't know how he'd gotten it—but refrained. "Seems fitting."

That he would change his mind and share this with her suggested he was making an effort to be more open, to have some semblance of a real relationship, despite what he'd termed his "limitations." She would've smiled at that but she didn't want him to think she was smiling at the fact that he was upset.

She leaned forward to peck him on the lips. "Are you going to give her the money?"

"Hell, no."

"I don't blame you." She started to get up, but he caught her arm.

"That's it?"

"What do you mean?"

"You're not going to ask me a million questions about Jo?"

God knew she wanted to. She was *so* curious about his biological family and background. But she figured he'd talk about his past when he was ready. She wouldn't try to force him to share things that were painful for him. "No."

"Because..."

"I already know the most salient points."

The old guarded expression claimed his face. "You're aware of what happened to me?"

She wished she could erase all the pain he'd suffered. She hated the people who'd hurt him, even though she'd never even met them. "I did an internet search."

"On *me*?"

"I was attracted to you from the beginning."

"My childhood is *on the internet*?" he asked with a scowl, obviously too fixated on that to react to anything else.

"You've never Googled yourself?"

"Why would I?"

"Some people do, just to see what comes up."

"I guess I've never been interested in seeing what's out there. Everyone around here knows me, so it didn't seem important until now. What'd you find?"

"An old article from when Aiyana first opened this place. They cited you and your...um...background as an example of the type of boy she hoped to help."

"Oh. Right." He relaxed a bit. "I have seen that article, now that you mention it. Although it's been a while."

"She probably needed the publicity to stay afloat."

"She tried to keep me out of it, but…there's no controlling what some reporters dig up."

"It made for a sympathetic story—a heartbreaking story—so it had to have helped with donations."

"I wouldn't know. I was just a freshman then. But… what you read about me, it didn't raise more questions?"

"It did," she admitted, "but I'm not going to pressure you for details. If you want to talk about that period of your life, I'm here. If not…let it go—if you can."

His mood lightened instantly. "Hallelujah," he said. "Let's get some breakfast."

Cora smiled to think letting him avoid that conversation would bring him so much relief. "At Lolita's Country Kitchen?"

"If you like that place."

She thought it would be a nice change to go out with him, to forget about trying to hide the fact that they were romantically involved. "Sounds good to me. But…what about Matt?"

He grimaced. "Don't tell me we have to invite him. I don't like him very much."

"No, we don't have to invite him," she said, laughing. "But I should at least go over and talk to him, tell him goodbye." And see what she could do to minimize the damage she might've caused by running out on him last night…

"Do that if you have to—then call me when you're ready," he said and tugged the sheet away to get a final look at her before rolling out of bed.

Eli's phone buzzed just as he was about to turn on the shower. He assumed it would be Jo again, but the screen showed Gavin's number, so he answered. "'Lo?"

"It's me. You on for basketball with the boys this morning?"

"Not today."

"Why not? It's Saturday. What else you got going?"

"I'm about to have breakfast with Cora."

A strained silence ensued. Then his brother said, "The same Cora who was at the bar last night with her ex-boyfriend?"

"Yeah."

"You don't find that a little strange?"

He leaned against the door to the bathroom while he talked. "They're just friends, Gav."

"I thought you were going to say *you're* just friends. That's the type of thing you normally say when I ask about a woman."

"Cora's different."

His voice changed, grew more somber. "Eli, I just passed Doug Maggleby a few minutes ago—out in his yard. He said her ex has been staying with her."

"I'm well aware of that."

"In a small house with only one bedroom…"

"Stop it. She has a couch."

"I'm just being real with you, man."

Eli started the shower so the water would get hot. "They're *friends*, like I said."

"How do you know?"

"She told me."

After another brief silence, during which he seemed to be weighing whether to continue the argument, Gavin said, "Breakfast with Cora it is, then. I guess basketball can't compete."

"You could join us."

"No. One of us needs to show up at the court. The boys will be disappointed otherwise. But…can I say one more thing?"

"I have the feeling you're going to do it regardless."

"I'll take that as a yes. Besides the fact that Cora's had

another man in her house for several days, are you sure you're doing the right thing, getting involved with one of the teachers here?"

"I'm not sure at all," he admitted.

"But you're doing it, anyway."

Eli remembered how he'd felt last night, right before she agreed to come home with him—and how having her say yes had changed everything. When he was with her he could more easily put his childhood into perspective, more easily remember the present and what his life was like now. "I can't help myself."

"That's freaking terrifying," he said.

Eli drew a deep breath. "Yeah, I know. I guess we'll see how it goes."

Matt was gone. Hallelujah! The dread in the pit of Cora's stomach eased considerably when she saw that his car was no longer in her drive. She still feared she'd find a nasty note waiting on her dresser, but at least she wasn't facing a confrontation.

After she let herself into the house, she held her breath as she wandered around. She was afraid he'd only stepped out to buy milk or something and planned to return. But everything that belonged to him was gone. And he hadn't left her a message or anything else to indicate that he was upset with her. While on the way home, she'd briefly considered the possibility that he might've dumped out her drawers, ransacked her personal belongings or thrown away her birth control...

Fortunately, all looked as she'd left it.

A ping signaled an incoming text message, so she reached into her purse to retrieve her phone.

Everything okay? Eli wanted to know.

Fine, she wrote back. She didn't think of her ex-boyfriend as particularly vengeful, but she did know he'd always been a little threatened by her search for her birth mother. He probably blamed the fact that she'd found Aiyana and was planning to move to Silver Springs as the reason she broke things off with him. It was easier to believe that than the truth—that she just wasn't fulfilled in the relationship.

Matt's not giving you any trouble? He's leaving?

He's already gone, she told Eli.

Great. Then I'm going to swing by the basketball court and play hoops for a while—until you're ready to go, okay?

The students were going to love seeing him. Okay. I'll walk over there when I'm done.

She set her phone to charge, since it was almost dead after going all night, and peeled off her clothes. Then she paused to stare at herself in the mirror.

"I hope you know what you're doing," she mumbled and turned on the water.

Chapter Sixteen

Jo tried to call three times and texted twice while he was at breakfast with Cora. Eli had believed, if he ignored her long enough, she'd simply go away. Now he wasn't so sure. His birth mother seemed determined, adamant—was desperate to get some money out of him. But she had no right to come to him in the first place.

"Have you thought about changing your number?"

The question caused him to glance up. Cora had seen him check his phone numerous times but, true to her word, she hadn't asked any intrusive questions. Although this one made it clear she knew who kept interrupting their meal, it still respected his privacy regarding the details of his past and his feelings toward his biological mother.

"I have."

"And?"

He set his phone aside. "Seems pointless to go to all that trouble."

"If hearing from her upsets you…might be worth it."

"I don't believe a new number would really get rid of her, not for any length of time. She knows where I work, could do the same thing she did before."

She drank a sip of her orange juice. "Which was…"

"She called the office, got hold of Betty May, gave a false name and claimed to be interested in making a large donation to the school. She even went so far as to claim that Aiyana Turner recommended she speak to me. After hearing Aiyana's name, Betty was so eager to make sure this 'donor' got through, she suggested Jo call my cell."

"Yikes."

"Exactly." He still hadn't had the heart to tell Betty she'd screwed up. He didn't want anyone to know that his past had come back to haunt him. He'd thought he could handle it, was determined to bear that burden alone so Aiyana wouldn't have to feel any added empathy or concern. She dealt with enough of that type of thing as it was.

"Has she ever come by—tried to see you in person?" Cora asked.

"Not yet. The last time she asked for money, she wanted me to use an app to transfer it. I doubt she has transportation."

"Where does she live?"

"I haven't even asked. I'm guessing LA, but it could be anywhere. Maybe she's out of state. I'm not sure what her situation is, to be honest. But chances are it's not good. It was never good when I was a child. I have no reason to believe that's changed, since it's obvious *she* hasn't."

He had to have raised more questions than he'd answered with the information he'd conveyed so far, but Cora simply said, "I see," and went back to eating.

"It can be so confusing," he admitted, watching her.

Her chewing slowed, and she swallowed. "What part?"

"All of it, but—" he pointed to his phone "—most especially what to do about her now."

"Parent/child relationships—even bad ones, *especially* bad ones—can be complicated," she said.

His food was getting cold, so he shoveled in a bite of his bacon-and-egg omelet. "Are you speaking from experience?"

"To a point."

"Care to elaborate?" he asked, waiting before taking another bite.

"Not really. I haven't experienced anything like what you have, which is why I hesitate to offer any advice. I don't appreciate it when people tell me what I should do or how I should feel about certain things when they've never been in the same situation."

He respected her for not being too heavy-handed with her opinions and remarks. That was what made it possible for him to talk to her even though he had so much trouble talking to most other people. He didn't have to worry that she wouldn't back off if he indicated he'd had enough. "I can appreciate that."

Cora put some jelly on her toast. "Does Aiyana know your birth mother's been trying to get in touch?"

"No. And I'd rather she not find out."

"Because…"

"Why upset her? There's nothing she can do about it, anyway."

"Do you ever hear from your father?"

"My biological father died in a motorcycle accident shortly after I was born, but he wasn't together with my mother, anyway. He probably wouldn't have been a big part of my life." Although… Eli had always wondered if it would've made a difference, had his father lived. "The man who married Jo and was there while I was growing up is in prison for sexually abusing his daughter."

She put down her toast without even taking a bite. "He had a daughter? Did she live with you?"

"No. Stayed with her mother, only came to visit once, maybe twice a year. But if she hadn't said something about me to the next-door neighbor—and that neighbor hadn't called the authorities—I might never have escaped my… situation."

"Seems more likely she would've told her mother about you. That didn't happen?"

"She was quite a bit younger than I was. Who can say how much she really understood or conveyed about what was going on at my house? The way I heard it, she said something about her father having a *boy for a dog*—as if it wasn't a big deal—which shows you right there that her understanding was limited. Anyway, Jenny's mother never did anything, even if she did know. I'm guessing she ignored what she could, felt the less she had to do with Tim and his life, the better."

"I bet she'd like to kill him now."

He turned his water cup around, making circles in the condensation. "That makes two of us."

"I don't blame you. Are you still in contact with Jenny?"

"She's married, lives in Virginia, so I don't see her often, but we've had lunch once or twice."

"And Tim?"

"Nothing from him, thank God. I wish my mother would follow suit and leave me the hell alone. I have a new life, am an entirely different person. I don't want anything to do with her."

She waited for the waitress, who'd come around with a pitcher, to fill her glass and leave. "So…what are you going to do?"

He picked up his phone. "I'm going to tell her to beat it. *Again.*" He did that, but turning her away wasn't as easy as he was leading Cora to believe. Part of him—the part that admired the mother/child sculpture Cora had brought into his office when they'd first met—still craved an apology, an explanation he could understand, some sense of closure, even a little contrition, if not a full acknowledgment of what she'd done. She owed him *something.*

Whatever that something was, however, he'd never get it. She was too narcissistic to feel the slightest bit of remorse. How could she feel bad about what she'd done when she claimed no responsibility?

As difficult as it was, he had to learn to live with the reality that she wasn't a fully functioning individual, that she never loved him and never would.

Some things just were what they were, he told himself.

"Is she or Tim responsible for the scar on your face?" Cora asked.

He fingered it, remembering. Late one night, he'd managed to get free of the cage they kept him in, but instead of running—he was too weak from lack of food—he tried to get something to eat. Tim caught him going through the pantry and slugged him so hard he'd flown across the kitchen, right into the door frame, splitting open his chin. There'd been so much blood, yet they'd never taken him to the doctor, which was why the cut had healed so badly. "Yeah."

Cora reached across the table to take his hand. "Bastards. I hope they rot in hell."

He couldn't help smiling. He'd never heard her use that kind of language before. "I like being with you," he said as if it was a revelation, because it was. Not only was she refreshing, she was *healing*, knew how to be supportive without being too overbearing. He felt like a whole new person when she was around, and that didn't happen with just anyone.

He expected her to say the same to him, but she didn't. "Who wouldn't?" she said and that enabled them to climb out of the mire of his past—to shove it all away—with a laugh.

Cora was invited back to Aiyana's for dinner on Sunday night. She'd been looking forward to it ever since she'd left Aiyana's house last week. Only this time she'd be going as Eli's girlfriend, which changed the way she'd be viewed by everyone else at the gathering. She knew Aiyana, and Eli's brothers, would be watching her in a different way. She'd also be that much more conscious of what she was hiding from them.

As it turned out, however, she didn't mind the extra attention. Gavin teased her quite a bit more and the younger brothers gave her shy smiles as if they were excited to think Eli had a romantic interest, but Aiyana treated her as kindly and politely as ever, almost as if she was determined to ignore the change. It was Eli who surprised her the most. He touched her freely and at every opportunity, despite the presence of his family. He could be so withdrawn and difficult to read, she hadn't expected him to be this demonstrative.

"How are your classes going?" Aiyana asked after they'd shooed the men from the kitchen so they could clean up without threading their way around so many big bodies.

Cora liked having this time alone with Aiyana, liked puttering around, helping with such mundane tasks. "They're going well."

Aiyana filled the sink with hot water. "You're not having any behavioral issues, are you? I remember you were worried about that."

"The new student—Zack Headerly—is giving me some trouble, but from what Darci says, he's acting out in English class, too. I think it's a general problem and not specific to me."

Aiyana lowered her voice in concern. "You know his parents were killed in a plane crash last year..."

"Yes. Eli told me. My heart breaks for him. That's why I haven't sent him to the office. I've been trying to gain a rapport with him, hoping the relationship we establish will encourage him to settle down."

"How's that going?"

Cora put plastic wrap over the cauliflower au gratin she'd made and contributed to the dinner. "It's too early to tell, but I remain hopeful."

"Let me know if you need help."

"I will. I was thinking that maybe Eli and I could take him and a friend riding this week. I feel as if some one-on-one time might help calm and reassure him. He needs to know that there are people who are still invested in him and his life."

Aiyana tossed Cora an approving smile. "That's the real secret," she said, her hands deep in suds. "I've invited him to have lunch with me tomorrow, so I'm trying to do the same thing."

Cora began loading the dirty silverware into the dishwasher. "Do you spend one-on-one time with all the boys?" That would be a daunting task, she thought, in addition to running the school and taking care of such a big family. Aiyana still had two high schoolers at home, who had homework every afternoon along with sports, but Cora supposed living on campus made a big difference.

"Just the most troubled," Aiyana replied. "I wish I had time to get to know them *all* on the same level, but the logistics are such that..."

"It's impossible," Cora finished.

"Sadly, yes." She raised a wet, soapy hand. "But enough about New Horizons and what's going on with the school. You're here to relax and have a good time. Why don't you tell me a little more about your family? I'm guessing you're missing them by now."

Cora did miss her family, although, once she got beyond that first night she'd been too caught up in adjusting to her new situation, fighting her attraction to Eli, making friends with Darci and feeling guilty for keeping her true identity a secret to get *too* homesick. "I've already been back to see them once. And I hear from them regularly."

"You're close to your parents, then?"

Cora hesitated before putting the glasses in the dishwasher along with the silverware. "Yes." Otherwise, she wouldn't feel so guilty for wanting to include her birth mother in her life.

"How's your brother doing?"

"He's been out of town. Claims he's going to come see

me when he gets back, but…he's always busy. Keeps putting it off. So we'll see. I'd love for you to meet him." In a way, that was true even though Cora knew she'd probably never introduce them—not with the way things stood now.

"I'm looking forward to that." She indicated the leftover carrot cake. "Any chance you'd like to take that home?"

Aiyana had obviously taken note of how much Cora had loved the dessert. "Sure. If you don't want it or want to keep it for the boys."

"We all get plenty of sweets as it is."

A ruckus broke out in the living room—Eli and Gavin wrestling with their younger brothers, who'd been teasing and goading them to get them to do just that. The loud noise and the rattle of dishes and other furnishings caused Aiyana to roll her eyes. "Boys."

"They seem to get along well," Cora said.

"Every family has its moments, but for the most part, they've been very good to each other. They are all wonderful people."

"They're lucky to have you."

Aiyana turned to face her wearing such an intense expression that Cora feared she'd given away too much with the longing in her voice. But when Aiyana spoke, she realized that Aiyana's thoughts were moving in a different direction. "On the phone just after you came here, you mentioned wanting to become friends with Elijah."

Cora swallowed with some difficulty. "Yes…"

"It appears the relationship has moved beyond friendship."

Feeling on the spot, Cora could barely refrain from wringing her hands. Like most all of the students and staff, she loved Aiyana, didn't want to displease her. "We are… we are dating, if that's what you mean."

"It's serious?"

"We haven't put a label on it. It's too soon."

"But you're open to getting serious with him."

When she flailed around, searching for the best answer, Aiyana dried her hands and moved closer. "I owe you an apology, Cora. This is none of my business, and Eli would be furious if he knew I was getting involved. It's just that I've never seen him like this. His eyes follow you wherever you go, and I think I indicated on the phone that as tough and unreachable as he may seem, at times, his heart is so fragile…"

After clearing her throat, Cora met her gaze. "Well, I'm just as concerned for my own heart, if that tells you anything."

Aiyana's face creased into a big smile. "For you, it wasn't quite as obvious to me, probably because I don't know you as well. So… I'm glad I asked," she said and pulled Cora into her arms for a warm embrace.

Cora breathed deeply, taking in the scent of her biological mother. She was hugging the woman who'd given her birth, a woman she was coming to love and respect more than she ever dreamed possible.

She probably hung on a little too long. When Aiyana tried to pull back, Cora couldn't quite let her go, but she didn't seem to mind. She kissed Cora's cheek—and then Eli interrupted by poking his head into the room.

"What's going on in here?" he asked.

Aiyana turned back to the dishes. "I just gave Cora the rest of the carrot cake, and she was thanking me."

"You gave her *all* of it? No way! I get half," he said, and later, once they were at his house, he decided to claim his share. But Cora didn't mind, since he ate it off her body.

"Were you really hugging my mother because she gave you the cake?" he asked as he licked a final drop of frosting off her nipple.

She caught her breath as he made sure he'd gotten it all, wondering if now might be a good time to tell him who she was. He'd just given her the perfect intro—and yet she couldn't bring herself to do it. What if their fledgling relationship couldn't withstand the shock wave?

She didn't want anything to come between them. Not only that, but Aiyana was so pleased they were together. Why risk ruining everyone's current happiness when she had all year? "Yes."

He dropped onto the bed beside her, seemingly sated and obviously tired. "Wow. You really like carrot cake."

"I really like your *mom*," she said softly.

"Doesn't everybody?" He propped his head up with his hands. "What's yours like?"

"She's…different from Aiyana. Not quite so socially conscious, but she's also a nice person. She did a great job raising me."

"You don't have any complaints about your childhood? The way you were talking at the restaurant, I thought maybe there'd been some problems."

"No big ones." Her mother's vanity could wear on her. Lilly could be a little materialistic, but Cora couldn't say anything derogatory about her. She already felt too disloyal just by being here—and getting involved in Eli's life and Aiyana's life…

"I'd like to meet her."

Cora wasn't about to invite Lilly to the ranch. She planned to keep this new world separate from the one she'd left in LA. Otherwise, she'd feel even guiltier. "She's really busy."

"Doing what?"

"She's a big philanthropist, always involved in one community event or another."

"That makes her sound caring."

Except that she sometimes gave the impression she did charity work more because she was bored and liked the positive attention it brought her. "She is caring. It's complicated, completely harmless. No one is all one way or the other, you know?"

"She doesn't have a job?"

"Doesn't need to work. But she has lots of friends she goes out with for…for brunch and movies and what have you. And she golfs," she added weakly.

"Ah, I can see she's completely buried."

Cora heard the sarcasm but pretended she hadn't. "She is."

"We're not that far from LA," he said.

"Yeah. She'll come visit. Sometime."

He lifted his head to give her a funny look. "I mean we could go there any weekend you choose."

"Maybe for Christmas," she mumbled since the holidays sounded a long way off.

He didn't say anything. He got up and went into the bathroom to turn on the shower so they could wash off the sticky residue of the frosting, and she leaned over to check her phone. She'd tried to reach Matt earlier, before going to the basketball courts to find Eli for breakfast, but he hadn't picked up. He hadn't responded to her text, asking him if he got home okay, either. She thought he was just going to write her out of his life, and was happy to have him do that. But when she took a moment to listen to the voice mail her mother had left while she was having dinner at Aiyana's, her blood ran cold. In a voice choked with emotion, Lilly asked her why she hadn't told them she'd gone to Silver Springs to meet her biological mother.

"Oh God," Cora whispered. Matt hadn't told Aiyana and Eli why she'd sought out a job at the ranch—but he had told Lilly.

Chapter Seventeen

"What did you say?" Eli poked his head out of the bathroom to see Cora grabbing her clothes off the floor and hurrying to get dressed.

"I said I have to go."

"But…you're sticky."

"I'll rinse off at home. There's been a—a family emergency."

Feeling a fissure of concern, he hooked his arms above his head using the lintel of the doorway. He would've helped gather her things, but she already had her clothes and there wasn't much he could do to help her dress. "What kind of emergency?"

"My mom…she's upset about something. I have to go home."

He turned off the shower. "Would you like me to drive you there?"

"No. It's fine. I'll go alone. I don't know when I'll be able to come back so…so you should stay here."

"Then…do you need someone to cover your classes tomorrow? If I can't get one of the other teachers to combine, I can always show them a movie or something—act as babysitter, at least."

Cora couldn't consciously leave her students in the lurch and make him step in, not when this wasn't the type of emergency Eli assumed. No one had been hurt or killed; no one was in the hospital. This was merely the consequences of the fact that she hadn't been able to let certain things go—things that some adopted kids, maybe even a lot of them, could do with apparent ease. "No. I'll be here."

"It's already eight o'clock!"

"The drive's only two hours. I can get there and be back before morning."

"After being up all night, will you be in any condition to work?"

"I'll muddle through. School doesn't last that long."

"I'm willing to help you," he said. "Just tell me what's wrong."

When she looked up at him, she had tears in her eyes, which brought him out of the bathroom. "Cora..."

"I'm fine." She put up a hand to ward off the comfort he'd hoped to offer. "I... I need to go. I'm sorry," she said and hurried out.

Eli stared after her. Just when he felt as if he was getting close to her, closer than he'd ever been to a woman, she seemed to retreat behind some invisible wall.

For a change, it wasn't him. But that didn't mean it wouldn't turn out to be a problem.

The silence in the kitchen felt tangible—like a thousand pounds of sand bearing down on Cora's shoulders, so heavy it was hard to bear up beneath it. Both of her parents were sitting at the table across from her, but neither seemed to have much to say. Lilly had cried a lot, and Brad acted confused, as if he was still trying to piece together why she'd needed more than what they'd provided when they'd given raising her their best effort.

"It isn't anything you've done," Cora reiterated. "You've been wonderful parents, and I'm grateful for everything."

He lifted his gaze to meet her eyes. "Then...why?"

She didn't get a chance to answer before her mother broke in, "Does your brother know? Did he help you?"

"No," she replied. "I only told Matt and Jill, because they were so present in my life during the past two years."

"And we weren't present?" she said.

Her father glanced at his wife as if he wanted to comfort her but was uncertain as to how to go about it.

"Of course you were," Cora said. "That's not what I meant. I would've told you, but every time I brought it up, you acted so...resistant to the idea—as if it would be a personal betrayal."

"So you did it, anyway," her mother said, fresh tears in her eyes.

"Not because it would hurt you! I never wanted to hurt you. I love you both. Why can't you understand? I *had* to meet Aiyana. A part of me has always been insatiably curious about her."

"What about your birth father?" Brad asked. "You're not curious about him?"

"I am but... I don't have any information on him. Unless Aiyana is willing to tell me the circumstances surrounding my conception, I have no hope of ever finding him."

"Will she give you that information?" he asked.

"I don't know yet. I haven't told her who I am. No one knows down at New Horizons." When she thought of Matt, she wanted to punch him. He had no business causing this wreckage. He'd only told Brad and Lilly to strike out at her, to hurt her for breaking up with him and having the audacity to find someone else.

"So when are you going to do that?" Brad asked. "And why haven't you done so already?"

"Because... I felt I should tell you first, for one. But the timing hasn't been right. There are moments when I think I'll never tell. At least I've seen my biological mother. At least I know who she is and what she's like."

Her father scratched his head, making his hair stand up. "I understand the questions you've had must've been... difficult," he said, making an attempt to be conciliatory.

"They were! I wasn't even certain of my nationality, Dad! Such a simple thing most others take for granted. I hated being so in the dark. I have only a partial picture now, but at least it's *something*."

"It's the deception I'm struggling with." Lilly glowered at her beneath wet eyelashes, but Cora wasn't convinced her "deception" was the root of it. Fear of losing Cora's affection was the real problem, which was probably why Cora had found her birth mother in spite of Lilly's resistance. She knew Lilly had nothing to fear. There wasn't any way her adoptive mother could ever lose her affection.

"I lied because there was no way of knowing whether Aiyana would be anyone I'd be willing to associate with. If she wasn't, I was going to leave things as they are now. I didn't see any point in upsetting you if I ended up walking away."

"But you're not walking away. You adore her!" her mother said. "You talk about her like she's Mother Teresa!"

"I admit the fact that she's such a good person makes everything a bit more…complicated, but it doesn't change how much you both mean to me. *You* will always be first, Mom. You were the one who stood by me when she walked away."

Fresh tears confirmed that Cora's comments had hit the real target.

"Mom, stop," she said, getting up to hug her. "How could you question my love for you? We've always been close, haven't we?"

"*I* thought so. I did my best by you, but I'm not the kind of person Aiyana has turned out to be. I'm no champion of orphans and abused boys."

"What are you talking about? You're always working on one fund-raiser or another," she said. "You do a lot of good. Besides, that type of thing doesn't matter. You've been everything I need. I have no complaints, so don't let Matt tear us apart. That's exactly what he intended when he called you. He's angry that I'm not getting back with him, so he's hurting me by hurting you."

Lilly wiped her cheeks, smearing her mascara. "I know he wasn't trying to do any of us any favors…"

"Have you thought about Aiyana and how *she* might feel about all of this?" her father asked.

"Of course!" Cora replied. "Why do you think I haven't approached her? I'm not attempting to force myself into her life—or anyone else's. I'm just trying to figure out who I am and where I came from."

"But Matt said you went home with her son last night!" Lilly said.

"Her *adopted* son. As far as I can tell, I'm the only child she's ever had."

"So that makes it okay to date him?"

"It's not ideal, but there's nothing really wrong with it. It's not like we're truly related."

Lilly accepted the tissue Brad got for her. "Then you're not worried about how *he* will feel when he finds out you deceived him,"

"Like I said, I'm not even sure he has to find out."

"That's not realistic," Brad said. "This is all leading *somewhere*, Cora."

And there it was—what scared them all, even her.

She took her father's hand. "Can you tell me why my birth mother gave me up, Dad?"

"No. They provided us with no information, Cora. We've told you that before. We were just glad to get you."

"And we didn't mind not knowing," her mother added. "We were excited to be your parents—your *only* parents. Having that blank canvas meant…it meant we didn't have to consider the fact that you weren't actually born to us."

"But the fact that I didn't come out of your womb doesn't matter, right? You've told me before. Only love matters."

"That's true," Lilly admitted. "You'd think that would

be enough, that you wouldn't have to go searching for someone who could…who would possibly ruin our lives."

"Aiyana can't ruin our lives if we don't give her that kind of power," Cora insisted. "The woman I've come to know would never want to hurt us, anyway. She'd step out of the picture before she became a problem."

"That's how you see her now, but you never know what she may be like once she feels entitled."

Cora rubbed her tired and burning eyes. "I'm sorry. I wish I could've been satisfied with not knowing. Maybe for some people, it's easy not to look back, to only move forward. But it hasn't been like that for me. I went to a lot of time, effort and expense to find Aiyana, and I wouldn't have done all of that if I hadn't felt compelled, from when I was just a little girl, to find out who my biological parents were—and why they gave me away."

Brad shook his head. "You hardly ever said anything!"

"Because I knew it would go like this!" she said.

"We would've tried to understand," he argued.

"Then try to understand now, Dad. Please? Wherever this is going, does it *have* to be somewhere bad? Can't I satisfy my curiosity, fill in the gaps that most people don't even think about so that I can feel satisfied? At peace? Can you trust my love enough to let me navigate my way through this?"

"Do we have any choice?" her mother asked.

"I guess not, since I've already done it," she said with a sigh. "But I'm an adult now. I feel like I should have the right to these answers. You know where you came from. Why can't I?"

They didn't answer.

"Still, I'd like your blessing, because I *do* love you and care about how you feel." She stared at them both imploringly. "Please?" she said again.

"You're *my* daughter. I don't want to share you!" her

mother burst out. "Especially with some…some saint I can't compete with!"

Brad took Lilly in his arms and Cora stood so that she could hover over her mother and rub her back. "But that's just it, Mom. You won't have to compete. *No one* can threaten your place in my heart. Ever."

"You're down there with her, aren't you?" Her mother's words were muffled—they'd gone into her father's shoulder—but Cora could understand them in spite of that.

"Only for the year." She sought her father's gaze and, when their eyes met, she could tell she'd managed to convince *him*, even if she hadn't been able to completely assuage her mother's fears.

"I want you to be happy," he said. "We both do."

"Then don't be mad at me for this."

"I don't want Aiyana in our lives!" her mother insisted.

"Mom, you'd really like her—"

"That only makes it worse!"

"Give your mother some time to come to terms with this," her father said softly, indicating that Cora should back down.

"Okay." She checked the time on her phone. "It's nearly two. I have to head back."

Letting go of Brad, Lilly whipped around to face her. "You're leaving? *Now?* But you can't drive for two hours. You haven't had any sleep!"

Cora wished Matt would've at least waited until the following weekend to sabotage her relationship with her parents. That slight adjustment in timing would've made it so much easier for her to recover. "I have a job, Mom. I have to teach."

Her mother grabbed her and pulled her into a tight embrace. "Don't go. I'm afraid you'll fall asleep at the wheel and crash."

"After such an emotional conversation, I'm pretty

amped up. I'll be fine." Perhaps it would be hard to get through the day tomorrow, but she figured, with enough caffeine, she'd manage...

Her mother cupped her face. "So you really like Aiyana's son? You told me he was intimidating."

"I didn't know him very well when I said that."

"And now?"

She smiled. "I like him. I like him a lot." *Too much*...

The promise of a possible romance seemed to check some of her mother's more negative feelings. She'd been after Cora for some time to settle down and get married so they could have grandchildren, since it didn't seem as if Ashton was in any hurry to provide them. "Will I get to meet him?"

"If you can be careful not to let on to what I'd rather they not know at this point..."

"I won't say a word," she promised. "That's up to you."

Cora slung her purse over one shoulder. "Then I'll bring him home with me next time I come—if he's available."

Her mother sniffed and used the tissue in her hand to dry her face again. "Make sure he's available," she said.

Cora chuckled at her sulky words. "Okay. He'll be my peace offering."

Cora was just getting her purse to head to the cafeteria to meet Darci for lunch when Eli ducked into her room. "Hey," he said. "How are you feeling?"

"Tired," she admitted, but smiled, anyway. She loved the way he looked in the worn denim jeans and soft T-shirt he wore. Because he was so involved in the school's athletics program—as well as caring for the school's animals—unless he had a business meeting he dressed more casually than the other administrators she'd known. But he did such a good job helping Aiyana run the school, and he fit in so well with both the faculty and the students, no one questioned what he wore.

"You got back late?"

Although he'd tried calling her around one to see if she was safe, she hadn't checked her phone until she was on the drive home and by then she felt it was too late to respond. "After four."

"Then you're running on almost *no* sleep."

She covered a yawn as she checked the clock on the wall. "I'm halfway through the day. I can make it."

He didn't pull her into his arms and kiss her like she was hoping he would. When he stopped halfway to her and leaned one shoulder against the wall, she was shocked by the degree of her disappointment, which only alarmed her further.

"So…what's going on?" he asked.

She busied herself straightening her desk so that she'd have a good excuse not to look at him. "What do you mean?"

"With your family. You seemed pretty upset when you ran out of the house yesterday."

"It was nothing," she said. "Just the usual stuff."

When he made no rejoinder, she glanced up.

"Stuff that you don't care to share with me."

Cora caught her breath. Was she being unfair to continue keeping her secret? Part of her was tempted to tell him, to completely unburden herself and let it out. But she was too frightened by what could change. He meant so much to her—already. And she couldn't begin to guess how it would affect Aiyana; she had no idea why Aiyana hadn't wanted her in the first place.

Surely there would be a better time to try to explain her situation—and that "better" time always seemed to be *later*. "Matt called my mother and tried to make trouble for me."

"By telling her you went home with me."

She cleared her throat. "Yes."

"And that caused a problem?"

"Matt and I were together for two years. She cares about him."

"She's hoping you'll go back to him."

Cora stacked some self-portraits she had yet to grade in the box of stuff she took home with her at the end of each day. "Not necessarily. It's just that… I've only been here a month or so. She was concerned that I might be jeopardizing my job." Part of what she said was true, at least. Her parents were concerned about what she was doing in Silver Springs—they were just concerned for different reasons than she'd given him so far.

"By hooking up with your boss."

"Yes."

"Does the fact that you're on the rebound have anything to do with it?"

"I'm not on the rebound," she said. "I'm over Matt." Sadly, she was over him before she even broke up with him. "But we were together long enough that my mother wasn't convinced of that. She expected us to get married one day."

He pushed off the wall and came toward her. "Why didn't you marry Matt? I bet he'd pop the question in a heartbeat if that was what you wanted."

"I wasn't ready. And I didn't love him as much as I felt I should."

He picked up the blown glass paperweight that had been an end-of-the-year thank-you gift from a class she'd substituted for and tossed it from hand to hand. "So did she calm down? Is everything okay?"

"Once I promised to bring you home for dinner."

No longer interested in the paperweight, he put it down as he came around the desk to where she was standing.

"Are you still interested in visiting LA?" She arched her eyebrows in challenge as he drew close. He'd mentioned driving her home to see her folks when they were in bed together yesterday afternoon, but meeting her family said something a bit more in this context. They both understood she'd be bringing him home as "her new man."

Her skirt moved up to her thighs as he lifted her onto the desk and stood between her knees. "What do *you* think?" he asked and pressed his lips to hers in a hot, wet kiss.

His hand slid up under the silky material while his tongue mated with hers.

"Eli!" she gasped when his thumb found its way beneath her panties. "Not here!"

"Shh…it's okay," he whispered. "Give me two seconds. Everyone's at lunch. Your back's to the door, anyway. The worst anyone will think we're doing is kissing."

That was bad enough.

"Meet me at my place after school, okay?" he said as he found and stimulated her most sensitive spot.

She could hardly think straight. "You mean after dinner? You usually work until six."

He ran his nose up her neck, breathing deeply. "Coach Sanders can get football practice started without me, for a change. I've got better things to do today."

"That will be okay? He—" she moaned as a finger joined his thumb "—won't mind?"

The way his pupils dilated and his body tensed made her worry he might try to take this further, but he didn't. "He won't mind. But you're right. I'm only making this harder on both of us." Pulling his hand away, he set her back on her feet as if he had to put her out of reach while he still had the presence of mind to do so. "I'll come up with some excuse," he said. "Then I'll join him for the rest of practice and let you nap. Knowing you're naked in my bed, waiting for me, will get me through the rest of the day."

Which meant he'd also come home to her after. Whatever she'd started with Eli, it seemed to be accelerating very fast.

Chapter Eighteen

Cora enjoyed getting to know her students over the next several weeks, despite facing some difficulties when it came to Zack Headerly. With Aiyana's help, she muddled through the challenge he presented and was actually glad for the opportunity to have something important to speak to her biological mother about. Trying to turn a specific boy around was a project they could work on and feel good about together.

The passing time brought other good things, too. She admired Aiyana more and more as the days went by, and she spent every extra minute she could with Eli. When they weren't together, she looked forward to his calls, texts and lunchtime visits. He often stopped by her classroom if he could. And, true to her word, in early October she took him to meet her folks, which went over well, except they liked him enough that they grew more worried instead of less about what might happen when he found out she hadn't been entirely truthful with him.

"That man's in love with you," Lilly would warn whenever they talked on the phone. But Cora would stubbornly refute that.

"He hasn't said anything about love," she'd argue. Although she longed to hear him speak those three words—had choked them back time and again herself—she was also sort of relieved. As long as he didn't make that verbal commitment, she could justify what she was doing by pretending their relationship wasn't that serious, that they were merely enjoying each other while she was in Silver Springs.

Jill agreed with her parents. "What do you mean he doesn't love you?" she'd scoff. "Of course he does! Maybe he doesn't come right out and say it, but he shows you in so many ways."

Jill, who'd seen them together twice and heard all the details of their relationship over the phone, was right. Cora had his full attention whenever they were together. He never acted like he didn't want to see her. They spent every night together, except for when he'd go out with his brothers or do something with his mother—or she was with Darci, Jill or her big brother, who met her in LA between trips to New York. Even when they split up for various commitments, he'd check in with her often and slip into bed with her after. In addition to all of that, he took her with him to Sunday dinner at Aiyana's every week. He even invited her along when he did extracurricular activities with the students, all of whom had come to view them as a couple. Some jokingly called her Mrs. T—or warned any new student that he'd better not flirt with "Eli's girl."

It was Thanksgiving almost before she knew it, and she and Eli were trying to figure out how to split their time between both families, just like a married couple. They ended up doing Thanksgiving dinner with Aiyana, the Turner boys, Aiyana's parents and one of her brothers—who were all so wonderful to meet—on Thursday and driving to LA to have dinner with her parents on Friday, since Ashton was hung up in New York and couldn't get back until then, anyway.

"He's quiet, but I love the way he looks at you," her mother said as they finished cleaning up after the big meal. Although Eli had helped with the dishes, too, he was now in the living room, watching football with her father and brother.

"You're making more of it than it really is," she said.

"We enjoy each other. But we know it's only a short-term affair."

Her mother stopped scrubbing the big roasting pan she'd used to cook the turkey. "You're still planning on moving back at the end of the year?"

"Of course."

"What about Aiyana?"

Cora did her best to act as though she had everything under control. "I've decided not to say anything—to just… let it go. That solves everything, right?"

"Does it?" she countered. "After everything you did to find her?"

Surprised that it was Lilly who was pressing the issue, Cora nibbled at her bottom lip. This almost sounded as if Lilly would *encourage* Cora to tell Aiyana the truth, even though doing so came with the obvious risk that Aiyana would accept Cora into her life and Lilly would no longer be Cora's only mother. "She didn't want me for a reason, or she wouldn't have given me up. And she must not regret her decision because she hasn't come searching for me."

Lilly turned on the sprayer to rinse the suds from the pan. "You don't know that she hasn't tried. Do you?"

"She could've found me. I found her, didn't I? And I had a lot less resources to work with."

"Maybe she's afraid you won't be happy to see her— that she'll disrupt your life. Or that she'll be stepping on my toes."

"I was facing similar questions and concerns, and I still fought to find her."

"I know, but from what you've told me, she's pretty focused on her work. Perhaps she *will* come looking for you someday when…when she's not so busy."

"I doubt it. Let's face it, 'busy' is an excuse. If I weighed on her mind as heavily as she once weighed on mine, she would've acted by now. Instead, no one even seems to know that she ever had a child." She stood on tiptoe to return a bowl she'd dried to the cupboard. "I guess, when you put all of that together, I have my answer. She *still* doesn't want me. But…at least we're friends. At least I know her. That fills in some of the blanks and helps to… I don't know…anchor me in some way." It especially helped that they thought well of each other. That was so huge, Cora couldn't regret having gone to such great lengths to find Aiyana. Thanks to the sacrifices she'd made, she'd had the opportunity to meet her grandparents and her oldest uncle yesterday, all of whom had been so nice.

"But you haven't been able to ask her about your father," Lilly said. "Or learn why she put you up for adoption. Both of those questions were important to you."

Those questions had helped fuel her curiosity, but she only had herself to blame for her current predicament. Although, in the beginning, her plan had seemed so clever, it had turned into a far-reaching lie that she was now hesitant to expose. "I've made such a mess of everything. I guess I deserve to remain in the dark. I should've been up front— with you, Dad and Aiyana—from the start. I was trying not to hurt anyone. I wanted to test the water first, but then I met Eli, and everything just…spiraled out of control."

"Have you heard from Matt since he called us?"

"To tattle on me?" She grimaced. "Yes. But just a couple of nasty texts."

"He sent you some nasty texts?"

"Only after I called him a jerk for telling you guys," she admitted.

"What'd he say?"

"That I'm not the woman he thought I was. Blah, blah, blah. He also said I should've told you to begin with. He's right about that one."

"But if you'd handled this any differently, if you hadn't

applied for a job there, you would never have gotten to know Eli. Maybe you would never even have met him."

"That's what Matt regrets," Cora grumbled. "He's mad that I've found someone else."

Lilly, who'd wrung out the rag and started washing down the counters, turned to face her. "I think you should tell Eli, Cora."

"About Aiyana?" She shook her head. "No. I've considered that many times, but I'm fairly certain she's never told him that she ever had a baby. I don't have the right to reveal something that personal about her life, in case,..in case it will somehow hurt her or what she's established." She retrieved the dish towel she'd been using before and started drying the wineglasses. "Besides, if I tell him, he'll feel like he has to share that information with Aiyana, for my sake if not hers, and I'd rather he not get involved, not be making those decisions for me." She heard a soft *ding* as she set another cup on its bell-shaped top. "So, no matter how I look at the situation, it comes down to the same thing."

"And that is…"

"I need to keep my mouth shut."

Her mother pursed her lips. "What if your relationship with Eli continues to progress? What if someday he asks you to marry him?"

"He won't," she said.

"How do you know?"

"Because he's a confirmed bachelor!"

A skeptical expression claimed her mother's face. "Surely, he'll want a family at some point."

"Why? A family isn't for everyone. He's told plenty of people that he'll never marry."

"Because he doesn't want to need anyone, doesn't want to be hurt again, right? But it's too late to protect his heart.

He needs you. And if he doesn't know that yet, he will soon."

She waved her mother's words away. "That's not true. The students at the ranch are his family. He's got his mother and brothers, too. And look at him—he could have about any woman he wanted if…if he was hungry for that sort of thing."

Her mother gripped her shoulders so that she had to look up. "I think you're underestimating him."

"You don't know what he's been through, Mom."

"Yes, I do," she said quietly. "You've mentioned a few things, so…your father and I looked him up on the internet."

Cora fell silent.

"It's tragic," her mother added in a whisper. "Does he ever hear from the people who…who were so unkind?"

"He hears from his biological mother every once in a while."

"He has a relationship with her?"

"No, he doesn't want anything to do with her. But she hits him up for money when she gets desperate." Jo hadn't called or texted him since he'd told her to leave him alone the last time, but how long would that last? She'd contact him again in the future. He said she reached out every once in a while, when she was desperate for financial support or she felt the need to justify her actions. He said she always tried to convince him that she wasn't to blame.

"How could any mother be like that?" Lilly asked.

"It's tough to imagine."

"Turned my stomach to read about it. But look how he's turned out in spite of them. I'm so proud of him."

Cora felt the same warmth pour through her she experienced whenever she saw him or thought about him. "So am I."

Her mother pulled her into a tight embrace. "I believe

you were brought together for a reason, honey. That it was meant to be."

"And Aiyana?" Cora asked.

Lilly released her. "I guess I'm finally coming to terms with the idea of sharing you."

She smiled wryly. "You just like Eli and know he wouldn't be part of our lives if I hadn't gone in search of Aiyana."

Her mother chuckled. "I admit that's part of it. Acquiring a son-in-law helps soften the idea that I might lose part of my daughter. But I've been doing some thinking—about you and me and the situation."

"And?"

"I've decided that I need to trust love," she said.

"What are you doing?"

Eli glanced up to see Gavin scowling at him for stopping so abruptly. They'd just finished breakfast, were walking down to the hardware store to pick up some parts Gavin needed to repair a sink in one of the dorms when Eli'd noticed they were passing H & G Jewelers. Sight of all the sparkling diamonds on display had caught his attention and caused him to fall out of step.

"Nothing." He pulled his gaze away from what was behind the glass so he could catch up, but turned back almost immediately. He wasn't ready to leave yet; he wanted to look some more. "I've been trying to come up with a good Christmas gift for Cora," he explained.

"You're thinking jewelry?"

"Most women like jewelry, don't they?"

"All the ones I know," Gavin agreed.

Eli gestured toward the door. "Do you mind if we stop in here for a few minutes?"

"Not at all." His brother followed him inside. "What

kind of jewelry are you looking for? A necklace? Earrings?"

It was the engagement rings that'd captured his attention. He'd begun to think about Cora in a different way. As easy and natural as their relationship had been, he'd felt the shift several weeks ago. He'd tried to fight it by giving himself all the reasons he'd be stupid to try to make it permanent. But no matter what he told himself, he couldn't seem to regain his enthusiasm for bachelorhood.

The simple truth was that he'd never cared for anyone the way he cared for her, never enjoyed someone so much. She didn't seem to mind that he couldn't verbalize his emotions or talk about his past, didn't take it personally. That helped, but there were other things about her that made her unique, too. She seemed more relaxed, more confident, more easygoing than any of the women he'd dated before. They just fit together somehow, and although she was still talking as if she planned to leave in the spring, he was beginning to dread the thought of going on without her.

"Eli?" Gavin prompted when he didn't respond.

"I don't know yet," he replied as a sales associate—a woman wearing a Santa hat—made her way over.

"Can I help you?"

"I'm looking for something special to give my girlfriend for Christmas," he told her. "Do you have anything you might suggest?"

"We have a lot of pretty things." She showed him a thick chain bracelet, a ruby heart necklace, some black onyx earrings and several other items. She had a good eye—he thought Cora would like any of the items she'd singled out. And yet his attention kept straying to that case of engagement rings he'd seen in the window.

Once he walked over there, the sales clerk quickly followed and smiled coyly when he met her eager gaze. "Or, if you really want it to be a nice Christmas, you could go for one of *these*," she said.

Gavin gestured dismissively. "Those are wedding sets."

"I know what they are," Eli said.

His brother blinked at him. "And you're still interested?"

Was he? For years he'd been adamant that he'd never tie the knot. But the four months he'd known Cora had been the best four months of his life. He'd never felt more whole or healthy in a psychological and emotional sense. The thought of presenting her with a diamond ring that showed he was not only willing but eager to spend the rest of his life with her was exciting.

It was also a little terrifying, given his past. He'd be launching out into uncharted territory. Would he be able to make her happy? Or would there come a time when things wouldn't be as easy or fun as they were now?

"Yes, I am," he told Gavin and, shaking his head at how quickly he'd fallen for her when he thought he could avoid love altogether, he pointed at a ring featuring a large round solitaire. "That one looks like her."

"Are you kidding?" Gavin cried. "That's a big diamond! It'll cost you ten thousand dollars, at least!"

The sales associate handed it to Eli, and he looked it over carefully. Unfortunately, the price was as high as Gavin had predicted, so he let his brother talk him into putting it back until he could devote some more thought to whether he really wanted to make such a purchase.

But over the next week, all he wanted to do was go back and buy that ring.

"Are you sure she'll say yes?" Gavin asked when Eli brought it up again while they were lifting weights one evening at the school gym. "Because every time I talk to her, she seems dead set on leaving Silver Springs as soon as school gets out. I mean, if she won't even stay here and teach another year..."

Eli had been a little worried about that, too. He knew she liked New Horizons and the area. She liked Aiyana, the rest of the staff, the students, too. And when she was with him? He got the feeling he meant a lot to her. Sometimes, just the way she looked at him seemed to speak volumes—especially when they were making love. But she'd never tried to commit him, never talked as if they had a future together. "I called the store this morning. The owner knows Mom, said I can surprise Cora with the ring and then return it if she says no."

"So you want to risk it."

He finished loading the barbell he was about to use. "The idea of proposing to her—of marrying her—has somehow taken hold of me, and I can't get it out of my head."

Gavin studied him closely. "You love her."

With a groan for the physical strain it cost him, Eli did eight clean and jerks before dropping the barbell. "Yeah, I do," he responded and realized that was the first time he'd ever said it out loud.

Chapter Nineteen

A week later, when Eli got up to play basketball on Saturday morning, Cora fell back asleep, so she was totally out of it when she heard a knock at the door. Eli didn't get many visitors. He gave so much to the school during the day that when he retired to his "cave," as Cora fondly called it, he demanded absolute privacy, and everyone knew it. That was what made it possible for her to stay with him so often. No one made a big deal about her almost living there because no one was privy to what he did, or who he spent his time with, after he disappeared from campus. Aiyana was about the only person who ever came over. Even Gavin and Eli's younger brothers typically called or texted him rather than showing up. So Cora wasn't surprised when she peered through the peep hole to find his adoptive mother on the stoop.

"Shoot," she whispered and waited, hoping Aiyana would realize he wasn't home and leave. Aiyana knew they'd been sleeping together, of course, but seeing Cora standing in *his* living room, wearing *his* T-shirt made it all a bit more...brazen, especially because he didn't welcome a lot of people into his house and she was becoming a regular fixture.

But Aiyana didn't leave. Another knock sounded.

Accepting the fact that she wasn't going to get out of this encounter, Cora used her fingers to comb down her hair and answered the door. "Hi," she said, squinting against the sunlight. Although Christmas was only a week away, the weather felt more like March or April.

Aiyana grinned as her eyes swept over Cora, then took in what she could see of the living room.

Nervously smoothing the wrinkles from Eli's T-shirt, Cora turned to follow her gaze. "What?"

"I've never seen this house look so...homey. My son actually has a Christmas tree—probably for the first time since he moved out of my house. And look, there're photographs of the two of you, and art you've created. Even a few plants. Wow. Who knew so much could change in such a short time."

"I tend to fill my space with the things I love," she said but flushed immediately after because this wasn't "her space."

"This place was pretty barren," she added lamely.

"So was his soul. Fortunately, that's changed, too," Aiyana said, but she didn't allow Cora any time to comment. "Can I come in?"

"Of course. Except Eli's not here. He's—"

"At the basketball court. I know. I tried calling you, but you didn't pick up so I decided to walk over."

Cora didn't get the impression she'd first tried the faculty housing. Aiyana had known right where to find her. "Are you...upset about something?" she asked as she stepped out of the way so that Aiyana could come in. Her mind raced through the past several days, searching for any incident in her classroom that might've warranted a visit from her "boss."

"Not at all. I'd like to go Christmas shopping today and was hoping you'd be interested in going with me. That's all."

Cora felt her eyes widen. "You mean...the three of us?"

"No. Just you and me. Eli's not much fun to take on an extended shopping trip. He's tolerant, if you know what you want and are just going to pick it up. But wandering around, admiring lights and decorations and such?" She shook her head. "Not particularly."

Cora laughed. She'd taken him to Rodeo Drive the last time they visited LA, since he'd never been there, and found that to be true. He was far more interested in seeking out places to eat or heading to the beach to play sand volleyball or go body surfing than shopping. "True."

"I thought maybe we could make a day of it, go to lunch, too. There's a delicious Thai place in Santa Barbara that I'd love to treat you to."

"I'd like that," Cora said.

"Great. How soon can you be ready?"

"Thirty minutes?"

"No rush. Just come over to my place when you're done."

"Sounds like fun." Cora was so excited about having the opportunity to be alone with her biological mother for hours—Christmas shopping, no less—that she grabbed Aiyana and hugged her on impulse. "I love you," she said. "You are *so* wonderful."

Although Aiyana permitted the hug, Cora could tell she was taken aback. When Cora let go, Aiyana searched Cora's face wearing a bemused expression. But then she smoothed the hair out of Cora's eyes and smiled. "I'm so glad you came to us," she said and kissed her cheek, just as she might've done had they been together when Cora was just a child.

Cora's heart was pounding when Aiyana left. She couldn't even make herself get ready. She sat on the couch, remembering every minute of that exchange. There was a moment when Aiyana was staring into her face that Cora had almost told her. She'd come *so* close…

She was still sitting on the couch in a bit of a daze when Eli walked through the door a few minutes later.

"Hey. What are you doing out here?" He used the bot-

tom of his T-shirt to wipe the perspiration from his forehead as he spoke.

Cora summoned the energy to stand. "Nothing."

His eyebrows came together as he dropped his shirt,
which was now stretched and wrinkled as well as sweaty.
"Was I gone too long? Have you been waiting for me?"
He checked the clock on his phone, which he'd left on the
counter. "I thought I'd wake you up when I got back. You
usually sleep until nine or ten on weekends."

"I wasn't getting impatient. Your mother came by and
woke me up."

He crossed to the kitchen to get a glass of water. "What
for?"

"To invite me to go shopping with her."

"Does she want me to go, too?"

"No. Just me." That was the beauty of it. Aiyana had
sought *her* out. She wasn't merely a tagalong because she
was dating Eli.

"Really." He eyed her speculatively. "Do you want to
go?"

"I'd like to—if you wouldn't mind me skipping out on
whatever we might've done today." They didn't have any
specific plans, but they'd started to spend all their weekends together, so she knew the expectation would be there.

"Of course I wouldn't mind, not if you think it'd be fun."
He downed his water. "So it's a girls' day, huh?"

"That's how she presented it."

"With as much as you admire my mother, I bet you'll
enjoy that. I don't get *any* attention when we go over there
on Sundays," he joked.

"You get plenty of attention—always." He was almost
all she could think about. If only he knew how drastically
he'd impacted her in every way. "But you're right, I'm excited to spend some time with her."

He walked over, took her hands and straightened the

rings she wore on three different fingers so that the jeweled parts no longer slanted to the left or right. "What is it about her?"

"Nothing," she lied. "I just...like her."

"I'm glad, because she likes you, too. Anyway, I'll take some of the boys riding. I promised those who scored the highest on Mr. Travers's chemistry test that I'd take them out one day."

Cora flinched beneath the guilt she felt for continuing to keep such a secret. "Perfect time to fulfill that promise."

Being careful not to get her sweaty, he leaned in for a kiss. "I'll miss you."

"I have a few minutes," she said with a promising grin and pulled him into the bathroom so they could shower together. She needed something powerful to help her forget the confrontation she knew was coming—eventually.

The day seemed so boring without Cora. That he missed her even more than he thought he would told Eli how much he was coming to rely on her company, which made him a little nervous. Would that turn out to be a bad thing?

If she insisted on leaving Silver Springs at the end of the school year it would...

He held off contacting her until it was almost dinnertime, hoping she'd get back. But then he texted her.

How much longer are you going to be? You guys are taking forever.

We're on our way home.

Have you eaten? Should I turn on the barbecue and grill a couple of burgers? He'd been waiting to eat with her.

No. I'm bringing you sushi. We had Thai for lunch but

ended up staying so long we went to sushi for dinner. It was a great place. You're going to love it.

Did you get all of your shopping done?

Most of it.

What'd you get me? he teased.

Nothing. I already had your present, she wrote back with a winking emoji.

Where is it? I'll go take a look.

You'd better not snoop around! You'll see it at Christmas.

He imagined how surprised *she* was going to be. I've got yours, too. Picked it up today.

I have no clue what it could be.

And she'd never guess. What he didn't know was whether she'd like it.

Christmas morning dawned to dark skies and rain. Cora listened to the soft patter hitting Eli's house as she watched him sleep. She cared so much about him, had never been so in love—and that meant she had to tell him the truth. Every minute they grew closer under false pretenses was a minute she feared he might one day hold against her. Aiyana, too. She'd been sleeping with him for *four months*. That was such a long time to perpetuate a lie, so long she'd definitely struggle to explain why she didn't speak up sooner.

But when she looked back, she couldn't isolate a point in time when she could definitively say, *That's when I should've said something.* As soon as she picked a point like that, she'd realize what the truth could've cost her—Sunday dinners at Aiyana's, the nights she'd spent in Eli's arms and the days she'd spent looking forward to them, the shopping excursion she'd enjoyed with her biological mother last week, being invited to Aiyana's for Christmas Eve. If she'd told the truth from the beginning, most of that, maybe none of it, wouldn't have happened.

Choosing the path she did had enabled her to create some beautiful memories. But if she lost Eli and Aiyana, mere memories would never be enough…

Eli opened his eyes and smiled the second he realized that she was awake. "Morning."

She returned his smile. "Morning."

"Merry Christmas."

"Same to you." She tucked her hands up under her pillow as she studied him. "Would you like to open your present?"

He covered a yawn. "We're not going to wait until we have dinner at your parents'?" They'd spent Christmas Eve with Aiyana and all his brothers last night so that they could join her family today.

"I'd like to give it to you now." Because it was something she hoped would speak to, and comfort, his inner child, she didn't want him facing an audience when he opened it.

"Okay." He sat up. "Let me have it."

She slipped out of bed to grab the box she'd put under the tree after they'd returned from his mother's house last night. Until that time, she'd hidden it in a closet at her place.

"It's heavy," he said as she put it in his lap.

"I hope you'll like it." She sat nervously on the bed beside him as he tore off the paper. "I mean…it's not something the typical guy would probably like, but… I don't know. It seemed to me as if…"

His expression changed, grew less anticipatory and more reflective, as he lifted her sculpture out of the box. Although it was conceptual, she hoped he could tell that it depicted a man holding the hand of a little boy.

"Wow," he murmured. "You made this?"

"I did. I admit I'm not as good as I want to be, but I was trying to create something for you that represented the difference you are making here at New Horizons—in so many lives."

"I love it," he murmured. "I've often stared at that sculpture you created of a mother cradling her child. That piece is the reason I hired you. I've always loved it."

"I've noticed. That's why I attempted this. If you like that one better, you can have it. I just thought it was more important to focus on what *you* are giving others." And not highlight the fact that he didn't at first have the kind of mother who would nurture him as a mother should.

"I don't even know what to say, Cora. This must've taken you hours and hours. I couldn't love anything more."

He seemed so sincere that she let her breath go in relief. "I'm glad. I struggled so long with the way their hands come together. That was the hardest part. It still doesn't look right to me."

"Are you kidding? That part—all of it—is perfect." He studied her gift for several more seconds before setting it reverently to one side. "And now I have something for you."

"You're going to give me your present now, as well? You can wait until we go to dinner, if you want."

"No, I think this is the right time."

"Okay." She felt such excitement. He'd bought her plenty of things so far—lots of meals and treats and even a few clothes when they'd happened upon a blouse or something she liked. She'd bought him stuff, too. But this was their first formal exchange. She thought maybe he'd purchased some art supplies or the painting she'd fallen in love with at the boutique off the beach they'd found last time they went to LA. But what he retrieved from his drawer was far too small to be either of those things.

It was jewelry. Clearly. But what kind?

She grinned at him as she tore off the tiny bow and the pretty wrapping. Inside she found a box with a lid. Under the lid was another box, this one the velvet type. "I never would've expected you to get me jewelry," she said. "We've never even looked at it."

He said nothing, just watched as she opened the lid.

Her jaw dropped the moment she saw the ring, and she blinked several times, trying to decide what it might mean. "This is…this is stunning!" she said. "Literally. I don't know what to say. It must've been *so* expensive. And…" And it looked like an engagement ring! She searched his face, trying to figure out if it *was* an engagement ring as he took her hand.

"Will you marry me, Cora?"

Cora could hardly breathe. This was a proposal— nothing she'd expected to come from Eli. Not this soon. He'd convinced her that he would never take that step, that he couldn't trust enough to take that step. Somewhere in the back of her mind, she'd always hoped he'd find his way around that barrier. But now? She wasn't prepared! She still hadn't told him the truth!

"You keep talking about moving away after next semester," he said. "But I hate the thought of that. I hope you'll stay here, with me. You gave me that statue to symbolize what I'm trying to do here at New Horizons—"

"What you *are* doing," she broke in.

"But you're doing the same thing—making a difference in the lives of young people who need you. *I* need you, too, even though I'm not so young," he added with a grin.

Her gaze met and locked with his. "Are you saying you *love* me, Eli?"

"How can you even ask that? Nothing else could ever make me take this risk. You've changed my life, Cora. Made me whole," he added softly.

Tears filled her eyes as she stared down at the big diamond he'd bought. "This is gorgeous."

He leaned in to catch her eye. "I was hoping you'd simply say yes. Don't you love *me*?"

"I do. Without question. I just…" She wiped her cheek with the back of her hand. "I have to tell you something before I can accept this. I wasn't going to do it on Christmas—I didn't want to ruin the holidays. But… I'm afraid I've put it off too long already. And now you'll hate me, which will make this ring a moot point."

Lines of consternation appeared on his forehead. "What are you talking about?"

She shook her head. "You won't believe it. And what makes it all worse is that I don't even know if I have the right to tell you. I feel like this should come from Aiyana, since you're her son. But…but it hasn't come from her. No one seems to know about me. And once I met you, I couldn't resist you. I tried. Lord knows I tried. Anyway, here we are."

He got off the bed. "That just confused the hell out of me. What are you talking about?"

"Aiyana's my biological mother, Eli." There. She'd said it.

For a moment, she wished she could snatch those words right back. She was so terrified of what they might destroy. But she couldn't continue to live a lie. That wasn't fair to Eli, which meant she didn't really have a choice.

"That's impossible," he said.

"I assure you it's *not* impossible. It's true."

"She had a child." His words rang with disbelief.

"Yes. One she gave up for adoption twenty-eight years ago—to a couple in LA. Brad and Lilly, both of whom you've met. I'm that child."

"But…why would she give you up? Was she too young? Unable to care for you? Aiyana loves children!"

"I can't provide the reason. She was twenty-one, so not outrageously young. That's the thing. I've always wondered why she didn't want me. That's what drove me to come here—that and wondering what my biological mother might be like."

"Does *she* know who you are?"

"No."

He shoved a hand through his hair. "Holy shit."

"I'm sorry, I would've told you sooner, but…it's all been so complicated for me. Once the private investigator helped me locate Aiyana, and I saw that she ran New Horizons and was looking for an art instructor, I believed it was meant to be. What an opportunity, right? I thought I'd apply and hope to land the job so that I could get to know her a bit before…before divulging my identity. I felt if I could only learn more about her, I might understand why she gave me away and be able to determine if she might welcome me back. That's all. I wasn't trying to trick anyone, not in a harmful way. And I certainly wasn't planning on falling in love with you."

He began to pace. "That's why you wanted the job so badly."

She nodded.

"And that's why you were so set on leaving at the end of the year."

"Yes. I didn't see any other choice." She sniffed to keep her nose from running. "As I said, it was never my intent to hurt anyone. That's partly why I haven't spoken up. Once I got to know Aiyana, I realized that there must be a good reason she cut me out of her life. But I've been afraid to find out what that reason is—even while curiosity eats me alive every day. Why would someone like Aiyana walk away from her own baby? It's been nearly thirty years— why wouldn't she come looking for me? And why has she never mentioned that she once had a child—*to anyone*? No one seems to know about me, which is why I feel guilty telling you. It feels disloyal to reveal all of this, as if I'm divulging her most intimate secret—even though it's my secret, too."

His chest lifted as he drew a deep breath. "Are you going to tell her who you are?"

"I don't know. I go back and forth on that every day— another reason why I never told you. I didn't want to burden *you* with the same uncertainty, didn't want you to wonder if you were being disloyal to your own mother by not telling, if that's the way you decided to go. So... I'll ask you the same thing—are *you* going to tell her?"

He sat on the edge of the nightstand. "I feel like I should—like we should do it together."

"What if she's not happy to have me back, Eli?"

"How could she not be happy about that? Look at you! You're gorgeous and so smart and good. What mother wouldn't be proud of you?"

At that point, the emotion Cora had been struggling to hold back got the best of her. As tears began to run down her cheeks in earnest, he walked over to scoop her into his arms. "Don't cry," he murmured. "It breaks my heart to see you cry. Everything's going to be okay. We'll figure it out together."

"You don't hate me?" she asked.

He laughed as he kissed the tip of her nose. "No. If this is the worst thing we ever have to get through—I mean between us, I understand it's been very difficult for you and I'm not making light of that—we're going to be okay."

"So are we getting married?" she asked. "Do I get to keep the ring?"

He reached over to get it. "Absolutely," he said as he slid it onto her finger. "Do you like this setting, or do you want to take it back and pick another one?"

"I want this one," she replied. Somehow it meant more that he'd gone to the trouble of finding what he thought was just the right thing for her.

"I'm glad you like it." He held her chin while he kissed her. "Merry Christmas."

Chapter Twenty

Eli was so happy that he and Cora were to be married that he tried not to let the little detail of her maternity bother him. He could see why she hadn't told him that she was Aiyana's daughter, so he didn't find it hard to forgive her. Being in love for the first time made him hesitant to let *anything* destroy the excitement they were feeling. He knew how wonderful Aiyana was, couldn't imagine her reacting negatively to the news, so he figured they'd wait until the holidays were over and sit down with her and explain everything. He told Cora that Aiyana probably didn't have the support she needed, so she'd made the decision to go with adoption because she thought it would be the best alternative for Cora—and had simply been too engrossed in helping others to search for her.

But the more he mulled over the situation, the more he began to think there had to be other factors he should be taking into consideration. Cora kept saying that the woman she'd come to know would not have walked away from her child unless she felt she had to. So, why did Aiyana feel she *had* to resort to adoption? And how could they find out before dropping a bombshell that could either make her incredibly happy, or bring up a part of her past she preferred to leave buried, even if it did include a child?

He didn't dare approach his grandparents or uncles with the conundrum he and Cora faced. Like Cora had said, it felt wrong to bring *anyone* in on this, especially Aiyana's family, since they didn't have her permission. But there was one other person Eli trusted, one person who also loved Aiyana with all his heart.

"Sorry for the delay," Cal said as he walked into his wood-paneled office, where Eli had been waiting for the past ten minutes.

Eli smiled as they shook hands. He believed Cal to be one of the finest men he'd ever met—and still it felt awkward to speak to him about something so personal. Maybe it would be easier if Cal's relationship with Aiyana had been more clearly defined over the years, if Eli felt as if he could look at him as a father figure instead of just a particularly generous friend of the family. But as much as Cal loved Aiyana, and Aiyana seemed to love Cal, the relationship had never progressed—a mystery in and of itself. "Thanks for seeing me."

"You said it was important."

"It is."

"What can I do for you? Do you need food, equipment, money for the school? If so, you came to the right place."

"Thank you, but…this has nothing to do with New Horizons."

Cal's ruddy face showed concern. "Then what's it about?"

"My mother."

A frown tugged at the corners of his lips. "I should warn you that might change my position. I care about you a great deal. I hope you know that. But my first loyalties will always lie with her."

Eli let his breath go in relief. "Thank you for confirming your devotion. That's why I'm here—because I knew I could depend on that."

"I don't understand."

"You've met Cora." Eli knew he had; Cal and Cora had joined them for several of the Sunday dinners they'd had at Aiyana's over the past few months.

"Yes. A very nice woman. You chose well."

"Thank you." News of their engagement had obviously spread, but Eli wasn't here to talk about that. He scooted forward. "I'd like to ask that what I'm about to say doesn't leave this room. If anyone is going to tell Aiyana about... what I plan to reveal, it should be Cora. Can you give me your word?"

"As long as whatever you're keeping from her isn't harmful to her."

"That's what I'm hoping you can help me decide."

Cal, more somber than Eli had ever seen him, leaned back in his seat and clasped the wooden arms of his leather swivel chair. "What is it?"

As Eli explained, Cal sat motionless, listening.

"You know Aiyana as well as anyone," Eli said when he was finished. "You love her, too. Should we tell her?"

"No."

Eli blinked in surprise. Cal hadn't sounded the least uncertain when he gave that answer. At a minimum, Eli had expected a bit of deliberation. "Because..."

"I'd rather not say."

Another surprise. "You need to tell me. Otherwise, I won't know how to protect *both* of the women I love."

"I'm glad you came to me before...proceeding. I'm sorry for Cora. She must've come to Silver Springs hoping for a happy reunion with her mother, but I'm afraid it's not that simple."

"Why?" Eli lowered his voice. "Was it rape? That's where my mind keeps going. What else explains such secrecy? Was Aiyana brutally attacked? Is Cora's father some scumbag rapist who's spent time in prison?"

"I think it would be easier for Aiyana if that was the case. Maybe then she'd be able to forgive herself. As it stands—" he shook his head "—no amount of atonement seems to be enough."

Eli's heart leaped into his throat. "Forgive herself for what?"

He didn't answer, was obviously still wrestling with his reluctance to break a confidence.

"Cal, as you've no doubt heard, in June Cora will become my wife. Please help me to understand the seriousness of this situation. Trust me to guard the secret as carefully as you have."

"I would if I thought it would help Cora to know…"

"But if she doesn't have a good reason not to, she'll eventually tell Aiyana who she is! The closer they become, the safer she'll feel to do that. And, as my wife, I can only imagine they will get close. That's already happening."

Cal dropped his head into his hands. "Aiyana will never forgive me."

"She'll never know. I swear it."

"Even if she learns, I care more about her than I do myself," he said on a fatalistic sigh. "So…if this might possibly protect her, I'll do it."

Eli could feel his heart pounding in his chest. "What happened?"

"When Aiyana was just a teenager, maybe eighteen, she fell in love with her stepfather."

A sick feeling crept into the pit of Eli's stomach. This was not what he'd been expecting. "She *what*?"

"He took advantage of her youth and inexperience, touched her where he shouldn't, convinced her they were meant to be together—and, eventually, she gave in to his entreaties and ran off with him."

"You've got to be kidding."

"I wish I was. She realized almost immediately that she'd made a terrible mistake, but by then the damage was done. She felt she could never go back. She'd betrayed her mother and taken away the father of her two younger brothers, was positive Consuelo would never be able to forgive her."

"So she stayed with him?"

"She had no choice, had nowhere else to go. They rambled around from town to town, picking up odd jobs and living in motels and dumpy apartments. Before too long, she was so miserable she began to search for a way out and finally met a girlfriend who offered to help. But when she tried to leave Dutch—Dutch Pruitt was his name— he came after her, made all kinds of crazy threats against them both. Your mother was so afraid he'd act on those threats, and hurt someone besides her, that she went back to him and, for the next year or so, was treated as more of a captive than anything else."

Eli's throat had gone so dry he could scarcely swallow. "How did she eventually get away from him?"

"She got a waitressing job. The owner of the place was a retired cop by the name of 'Murph' Matheson, and he and his wife took a shine to her. They helped her get a restraining order against Dutch, let her move in with them and their children. They even insisted she start college and helped with the expenses."

"And the pregnancy?"

"Your mother realized she was going to have a baby a month after she moved in with the Mathesons. But she knew if she kept the baby, she'd never really be rid of Dutch. He'd be part of her life forever, and because she was convinced he wasn't completely sane she didn't want him around the baby. She also knew her mother would never be able to accept the child, would never be able to love it, if they ever reconciled, which was something she was beginning to hope for. So…"

"She gave it up."

"That's right."

Leaning back, Eli took a deep breath. "Did Dutch ever find out about the baby?"

"No. But he would have had she kept it. It took another three years for her to get rid of him altogether. He was a truck driver by then and took his own life by driving his semi over a cliff."

Eli sat rubbing the beard growth on his chin as he attempted to process this information. "Wow..." he said on a long exhale. Even a saint like his mother had a skeleton in her closet, and that skeleton had quite a stigma attached to it.

Cal came to his feet and circled the desk. "Eli, I hope you won't let this damage your opinion of your mother. I would feel terrible if it did. Regardless of her past, I've never met a better person. I don't think she should be defined by that one mistake."

He lifted a hand to signal that Cal had nothing to worry about. "I'm not judging her," he said. "My mother has proven who she is many times over." This just confirmed, once again, that no one was perfect.

But what did he do with the information now?

While Eli was gone, Cora cooked some Cajun pasta sauce for their dinner from a recipe she found on the internet. She was trying to stay busy, but she often found herself staring off into space, wondering if Cal might be able to answer some of the questions that'd nearly driven her mad over the years—and if Eli was getting him to talk. Would Cal know that his beloved Aiyana had had a child? And, if so, had Aiyana told him she'd put that child up for adoption?

Even if he *didn't* know, if the news came as a complete surprise, would he suggest they tell Aiyana who she was—or not?

Cora would've gone to see Cal along with Eli, so that she could take part in the discussion. She really wanted to be there. But Cal was so protective of Aiyana, she and Eli both felt that Eli had a better chance of getting him to open up without her—which left her to wait and worry.

Although Eli was gone for only a couple of hours, it felt like forever. The second Cora heard him at the door, she turned off the stove, left the Cajun sauce in the pan and hurried to meet him. "How was it?" she asked as he came in.

That Eli didn't seem to be relieved or excited made Cora's chest constrict to the point that she could barely breathe. She tried to read his thoughts and feelings as he grimaced and rubbed his forehead.

"It wasn't good," she surmised.

He pulled her over to the couch. "I think maybe you should sit down."

She did as he suggested but perched on the very edge, too nervous to relax. "Cal didn't know anything about me?"

"Actually, he did."

She wanted to feel some hope, but Eli's manner didn't warrant any. "And…"

"It's complicated—difficult to know how to proceed without hurting Aiyana as well as…others."

"Others?" she echoed in surprise.

"That's the thing. This could affect more than just you and her."

"Do you mean Lilly and Brad? Because they're okay with me telling Aiyana. They weren't at first. They felt threatened, to a degree. You know that. But they've begun to understand that I'm an adult now, and I should have the right to know where I come from. They also know it won't change how I feel about them."

"I'm not talking about Brad and Lilly, Cora."

She drew a deep breath and clasped her hands together to stop them from trembling. "Then who?"

He wore a sympathetic expression as he reached over to slide a strand of hair out of her eyes. "Remember how you had trouble telling me that you were Aiyana's child because no one knew she even had a child and you thought you might be revealing something too personal?"

Cora curled her fingernails into her palms. "Yes..."

"That's how I feel right now. What happened to Aiyana, what she did, would be hard to...to cope with. She's not completely to blame—she was so young—but she made some bad decisions that got her into a situation no one would ever ask to be in."

"She was raped?" Cora had wondered that before, many times. If Aiyana had been raped, Cora could understand why she might not care to live with the reminder, so she was surprised when he shook his head.

"No. Cal said, and I agree, that if it had been a random attack, something where she wasn't also culpable, she might've been able to get over it by now."

"You're saying she's *not* over it."

"Not from what I can see. If she was, I believe she'd be married to Cal. Instead, she's pushing him away, denying herself any hope of that kind of happiness and fulfillment."

"She's punishing herself because of *me*?"

"Not because of you. Because of guilt. Because of regret. Because she hurt someone she loves. Cal told me she doesn't believe she deserves to be happy, which is why we see her giving so much to everyone else while continually denying herself."

"*Cal* said that?"

"Not in so many words. But once he explained the situation, I understood. Aiyana's rejecting his love because she doesn't feel she deserves it."

Forcing her hands open, Cora rubbed her sweaty palms on her denim-clad thighs. "But if it wasn't rape, how bad can it be? And if it *is* that bad, why would Cal ever open up about it?"

"Trust me, he was reluctant. He just didn't have much choice, not with you living here and marrying me."

"Your mother wouldn't want me here if she knew who I was. That's the bottom line, isn't it?" She'd told herself she'd accept whatever Eli came back with, take it well. She'd been lucky enough to have Lilly and Brad. But she couldn't stem the bitter disappointment that flooded through her.

"*I* don't believe that, no. And it took some convincing, but before I left Cal agreed with me. As painful as it might be, confronting the truth is the only way you'll be able to have the relationship with Aiyana that you deserve, and then maybe she can finally heal. Sometimes things have to get worse before they can get better."

Those were harrowing words. "So what is it?" Cora asked. "You're going to tell me, right? What happened?"

Eli seemed to have trouble getting started. Whatever Aiyana had done was obviously not something he wanted to expose.

"Eli?" she prompted.

Finally, he managed to explain what'd happened nearly thirty years ago. He did so as diplomatically and kindly as possible, but what he had to say still shocked Cora.

"Wow," she said when he was finished.

"She was young, confused," he added for the second or third time. "What she did is so unlike her. There must've been some extenuating circumstances that we're not aware of."

Cora's mind raced as she tried to imagine how a situation like that could've developed and the damage it would cause. "My heart aches for her as much as it does Consuelo and her younger brothers. No wonder Aiyana doesn't have much of a relationship with those two."

"I'm guessing Consuelo has forgiven her. But I feel like those two brothers might be harboring some resentment, which is why I've hardly ever seen them."

"So what did you mean, it's time for the truth to come

out? We can't tell your mother who I am, Eli. If not for me, she'd be able to leave the past in the past, which is something she's proven she's desperate to do. I love her, too. I didn't come here to bring her misery and unhappiness."

"That's just it," he said. "Once you sit down and tell her who you are—"

"No! Aren't you listening? I don't want to serve as a constant reminder of—of all that."

Eli scooted closer. "Hear me out. Why not tell her and leave it there? I mean, just because you both know doesn't mean *everyone* else has to know."

Her mind raced as she tried to comprehend what he was getting at. But she was still processing The Terrible Secret in which she played such an integral part. "You're suggesting we tell her but not the extended family?"

"Or anyone else. Why would we have to? You'll soon be her daughter-in-law as well as her daughter. If she loves you, spends a lot of time with you, calls you her little girl, no one will think twice about it, even Consuelo or my uncles. From what Cal told me, Consuelo never knew about the pregnancy. Aiyana went through those nine months, and the delivery, alone. She made the decision to put you up for adoption alone, too. Then she did her best to move on and build something out of her life—and she did that alone, too, until she could reconcile with her family, which didn't happen until about five years after you were born."

"She didn't tell *anyone*?"

"Only Cal, and that well after she was back in touch with her family. He said she couldn't talk about those years or the adoption without breaking down. She was too ashamed. And she didn't want to hurt her mother and brothers any more than she already had by announcing the fact that she'd had a baby by her former stepfather."

Cora nibbled at her lip as she pictured what having such a discussion with Aiyana might be like but eventu-

ally shook her head. "I can't. I can't tell her if she'll only
be sad that I found her. That's not why I came here."

"Cora, listen to me." He took her hands. "Imagine how
she must feel when she thinks of you. She gave you up because she was convinced she had to, which means, not only
did she lose her family, at least for a while, she lost her
only child. That *has* to be painful. She feels she deserves
the pain, which is why she's tried so hard not to look back
and hasn't taken up a search for you. But if you were to
come to her, and it didn't hurt her mother, her brothers or
anyone else, I have to believe it might finally fill the hole
in her heart. Don't you see? Finding out that her baby had
a good upbringing, one in which she was treated well, and
has turned into such a beautiful, fully functioning young
woman would *have* to erase some of that terrible guilt. It
would also make her proud. Having you back... I believe
she'd feel complete—at last."

Cora's eyes began to burn with unshed tears.

"You *have* to tell her," he said. "Only you can bring
her peace."

Cora almost turned around a million times. If not for
Eli's words, his strong belief that she was doing the right
thing, she would have. Instead, early the following Sunday,
after a sleepless night she spent alone at her own house, she
kept walking toward Aiyana's. At least she knew that Liam
and Bentley wouldn't be there, that she and her biological mother would have the house to themselves. When Eli
had called Aiyana to set up this appointment, he'd asked
if the boys could spend the night with him. According to
the good-luck text she'd just received from him, Liam and
Bentley were still sound asleep. She knew Eli would run
interference for her until he received the "all clear."

Everything was ready—except her.

"How am I going to say it?" she muttered as she trudged along, hugging herself against the early morning chill.

Fortunately, the campus was deserted. She was grateful for that, wasn't sure she'd be able to fake a smile if she happened upon a student or fellow teacher. She was close to tears, and she hadn't even arrived yet.

When she did reach Aiyana's, Aiyana answered the door immediately. Cora could tell she'd been waiting and watching for her. Aiyana knew something serious was up; the concern in her eyes proved it.

"Thanks for...thanks for allowing me to come over," Cora said.

Aiyana stood aside and waved her in. "Of course. You're welcome here anytime. I hope you know that."

"I do."

Aiyana led her into the living room where that picture of Hank, Consuelo and family graced the old piano. Cora felt a niggle of doubt when she glanced at it. Once she said what she had to say, there'd be no taking it back. But she knew she'd come too far to change her mind. For better or worse, it was time for the truth.

"Why all the secrecy?" Aiyana asked as they sat, facing each other, on the sofa. "I'd assume it was because you want to arrange a surprise for Eli, maybe for the wedding, but he's the one who asked me to set this time aside and insisted on taking the boys, so...that doesn't seem to fit."

"No, it's not that kind of surprise."

"So he knows what you're about to say."

"He does. Cal does, too. And my parents. They all felt you and I should address this at a time when we could be alone and weren't likely to get interrupted."

Her eyebrows knit above her dark, searching eyes. "*Cal's* part of this?"

"Yes. And my parents, as I said. But it's a very small,

tight circle, and we all want what's best for you. This is no one else's business but our own."

The color drained from Aiyana's face as she stiffened. "You're giving me the impression this is bad news. You and Eli haven't changed your mind about the wedding. You're not leaving New Horizons."

"No. I love Eli more than I've ever loved anyone. I hope I'll be able to make him happy."

"I know he feels the same about you. You've taught him to trust again. I've been waiting for a woman to come along who had the power to do that. So…"

Cora couldn't help wringing her hands. "Aiyana, I… I'm…" She tapped a hand to her chest as if she could force out the rest of the words, but that was as far as she got before she choked up and couldn't speak.

Sympathetic tears filled Aiyana's eyes. "What is it, Cora?" she asked. "You can tell me anything."

"It's something I've been trying to tell you since I came here. Since the private investigator who…who helped me first find you."

With a gasp, Aiyana covered her mouth. She knew. In that moment, she knew, but Cora spoke, anyway.

"I'm the child you gave up."

"Twenty-eight years ago," she whispered, her eyes filled with nostalgia and pain. "Twenty-nine on February 21."

"Yes. I—I hope you're not upset that I went to such great lengths to find you. And that I didn't tell you from the start. I'm not here to remind you of anything that might be painful or to bring you any unhappiness. I just… I've always craved a connection. And now that I have one, I'm glad. You are everything I ever hoped you would be!"

She sprang to her feet and backed away as if Cora had slapped her. "No, you have no idea who I really am. What I…what I did."

Cora stood, too, and caught hold of her hands. "That's just it, I *do* know. And it doesn't change anything."

A tortured expression claimed her face. "But I'm so ashamed—"

"Don't be," Cora broke in. "Let it go. All the people you know love you in spite of whatever you did in the past. I want to share my life with you as the daughter I am. But as far as I'm concerned, your mother, the rest of your family, everyone else can know me as your daughter-in-law."

"I won't ask you to lie for me," Aiyana said.

"You're not asking me to lie. We'll keep this to ourselves for their sakes. Why would they need to know? Why open that old wound? They never knew I existed in the first place, so they aren't missing anything. I'm perfectly satisfied with that and would be thrilled if only...if only you could forgive yourself and let yourself love me in return."

"I *do* love you," Aiyana said. "I have never forgotten the day you were born. I can't tell you how many millions of times I've thought of you and wished...wished I could at least know where you were, if you were happy, if you had what you needed."

Which was why she'd made it her life's mission to love every orphaned child she could, why she'd adopted so many. Cora could easily see the correlation—her attempt to compensate. "The past is the past. It can't be changed. Just don't deny us a future. Please?"

"I never would." Aiyana squeezed her hands. "I can't believe I have you back, that nearly thirty years of wondering and worrying has come to an end."

Cora smiled through her tears. "Thank you."

"No, thank *you*." She pulled her into a tight embrace. "I'll never let you go again."

Epilogue

"What do you think of this?"

Cora turned to see Aiyana holding a lovely teal bridesmaid dress. Although she'd done most of her wedding shopping in LA with Lilly—who'd made it her new life's mission to throw the most spectacular wedding in the world and had dived in as if they'd given her only six weeks instead of a full six months to plan everything—they'd been unable to find the right bridesmaid dresses. Cora had been hoping to visit Santa Barbara to see if she could find anything different, so she'd invited Aiyana to drive over with her and have lunch.

"Oh my gosh! That's it!" she exclaimed. "Finally! Do you know how many shops I've visited?"

"More than ten?"

"More than twenty!"

"Lilly must've loved such an in-depth hunt."

Cora smiled at the sparkle in Aiyana's eyes. They both knew how much her adoptive mother enjoyed shopping. "She did. I'm sure she'll be slightly disappointed that we came up with this on our own."

"I'll have to tease her about that," Aiyana joked.

"It's a good thing she likes you."

"I never realized that by getting my daughter back, I'd also be getting such a good friend."

They checked the price, sent Lilly a picture and, after receiving her exuberant reply, ordered one in the appropriate size for Jill, Darci, an old childhood friend who Cora kept in touch with every few months, two other friends from high school and a teacher she'd met while substituting at Woodbridge High.

"Well, it's exciting to finally meet with success, but finding the dress so early cuts our day short," Cora said as they left the boutique. "I didn't expect to buy from the first shop we visited."

"We can start searching for something else on the list. What's left?"

"My shoes. I haven't yet found a pair that's both pretty and comfortable. But the restaurant's just down the street, so let's eat before we do any more shopping. I'm starved."

"Me, too." As Aiyana linked her arm through Cora's, Cora felt such a tremendous rush of love and admiration. Her relationship with her biological mother was every bit as good as she'd ever dreamed it could be.

"Thanks for taking the time to come with me today," she said.

"I love being included, love having you in my life. I can't wait for the wedding."

Cora covered her mother's hand as they sauntered down the sidewalk. "We could always make it a double wedding, you know."

Aiyana pulled Cora to a stop. "What are you talking about?"

"Me and Eli—you and Cal."

A blush suffused Aiyana's cheeks. "What makes you think I'd ever marry Cal? We're just friends."

"It's hilarious you'd even try to say that!" Cora said, laughing. "I know you stayed over at his place last Friday, when we had Bentley and Liam."

Her cheeks, already red, turned crimson. "I got home late, that's all."

Cora couldn't quit grinning. "Uh-huh."

"How'd you know?" her mother asked.

"Liam forgot something, so we dropped by the house. Your car wasn't there."

"Liam doesn't know I slept at Cal's, does he?" she said with a gasp.

"He didn't even seem to notice that your car was gone. He was too preoccupied with getting the video game he wanted. And Eli and I didn't talk about it until later, after the boys were asleep."

"I can't get away with anything," she grumbled.

Cora laughed again. "Which brings me back to the idea of a double wedding…"

Seemingly flustered, Aiyana waved her off. "Don't even suggest that! We would never horn in on your happiness."

"You wouldn't be 'horning in.' We'd be thrilled to share the limelight."

"You're jumping to conclusions." Aiyana started to walk away from her, picking up the pace as if she could outdistance the conversation, too. "Let's not even talk about it."

Cora hurried to catch up with her. "He loves you, you know." And the two of them had grown so much closer in the last few weeks. Eli had noticed the same thing.

"I'm too old for that sort of thing," she insisted.

"That's what you always say. But I think you should reconsider your stance—to allow yourself to be happy at last."

Aiyana stopped again and pivoted to face her. "He's mentioned it," she suddenly admitted, sobering.

Cora felt her eyebrows slide up. "And?"

"I'm not ready. But—" her lips curved into a rather shy smile "—maybe soon."

"That's wonderful!" Cora cried.

She lifted a hand. "Like I said, let's not talk about it now. Your wedding comes first. After that's over, in another year or so, I don't know. We'll see."

Aiyana had already revealed far more than Cora had

expected, so she let her retreat behind her usual curtain of privacy and they talked about other things as they walked the final block. Just before they entered the restaurant, however, Aiyana stopped Cora and, to Cora's surprise, hugged her. "Eli's so lucky to have found you."

Cora stared up at the beautiful spring sky visible over her mother's shoulder, grateful that she was finally satisfied and not still questioning, wondering and searching. "And we're both lucky to have you."

* * * * *

*Don't miss the next book
in the* SILVER SPRINGS *series,
NO ONE BUT YOU
available soon from MIRA Books*

Dear Reader,

This month—April 2017—marks the 35th anniversary for Harlequin Special Edition! Perhaps it's as hard for you, the reader, to believe this as it is for us, the team that has been presenting this warm, wonderful and relatable series of books for all these years. And while some of us are newer than others, the one thing that has always been consistent is that the Harlequin Special Edition lineup has always reached out and grabbed you, made you want to read more, made you look forward to what comes next.

April 2017 is a great illustration of this. We have *New York Times* bestselling author Brenda Novak in Harlequin Special Edition for the first time with *Finding Our Forever*, alongside our almost-brand-new author Katie Meyer with another in her Proposals in Paradise series, *The Groom's Little Girls*. We have *USA TODAY* bestselling and beloved authors Marie Ferrarella (*Meant to be Married*) and Judy Duarte in our next Fortunes of Texas: The Secret Fortunes story (*From Fortune to Family Man*). And if it's glamour, glitz and sparkle you want with your romance, look no further than *The Princess Problem* (next in the Drake Diamonds trilogy) by Teri Wilson.

We have moved through the last thirty-five years giving you, the reader, stories that warmed your heart and curled your toes, and we are just getting started! So happy anniversary...and here's to the next thirty-five!

Happy Reading,

Gail Chasan
Senior Editor, Harlequin Special Edition

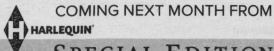

*When Sheriff Seth Yancy finds out Jody Bravo is
pregnant with his late brother's child, he's determined
to stay in their life, even if that means making her a very
convenient bride...*

Read on for a sneak preview of
THE LAWMAN'S CONVENIENT BRIDE,
the next book in New York Times
bestselling author Christine Rimmer's,
THE BRAVOS OF JUSTICE CREEK *miniseries.*

"Mirabelle's?" It was a new restaurant in town, a small, cozy
place with white tablecloths and crystal chandeliers and a chef
from New York. Everyone said the food was really good and
the service impeccable.

"I heard it was good," he said. "Would you rather go
somewhere else?"

"I just didn't know we were doing that."

"Doing what?"

"Going through with the date."

He set down his fork. "We're doing it." His voice was deep
and rough, and his velvet-brown gaze caught hers and held it.

It just wasn't fair that the guy was so damn hot. *Not
happening*, she reminded herself. *Don't get ideas.* "What about
Marybeth?"

"It's only a few hours. Get a sitter. Maybe one of your sisters
or maybe your mom?"

"Ma? Please."

"She did raise five children, didn't she?"

"She's probably off on her next cruise already."

"A babysitter, Jody. I'm sure you can find one."

"But Marybeth is barely four weeks old."

"Jody. We're going. Stop making excuses."

She sagged back in her chair. "Why are you so determined about this?"

"Because I want to take you out."

"But…you don't go out, remember? There's no point because it can't go anywhere. Not to mention, I live in Broomtail County, and what if it got messy with me?"

"Too late." He was almost smiling. She could see that increasingly familiar twitch at the corner of his mouth. "It's already messy with you."

"I am not joking, Seth."

"Neither am I. I want to be with you, Jody. And not just as a friend."

"B-but I…" God. She was sputtering. And why did she suddenly feel light as a breath of air, as if she was floating on moonbeams? "You want to be with me? But you don't do that. You've made that very clear."

"You're right. I didn't do that. Until now. But things have changed."

"Because of Marybeth, you mean?"

"Yeah, because of Marybeth. And because of you, too. Because of the way you are. Strong and honest and smart and so pretty. Because we've got something going on, you and me. Something good. I'm through pretending that we're friends and nothing more. Are you telling me I'm the only one who feels that way?"

"I just…" Her pulse raced and her cheeks felt too hot. She'd promised herself that nothing like this would happen, that she wouldn't get her hopes up.

She needed to be careful. She could end up with her heart in pieces all over again.

Don't miss
THE LAWMAN'S CONVENIENT BRIDE
by Christine Rimmer, available May 2017 wherever
Harlequin® Special Edition books and ebooks are sold.

www.Harlequin.com

$7.99 U.S./$9.99 CAN.

$1.⁰⁰ OFF

New York Times
bestselling author
brenda novak

welcomes you to Silver
Springs, a picturesque small
town in Southern California
where even the hardest hearts
can learn to love again…

Available May 30, 2017.

$1.⁰⁰ OFF the purchase price of NO ONE BUT YOU by Brenda Novak.

Offer valid from May 30, 2017, to June 30, 2017.
Redeemable at participating retail outlets, in-store only. Not redeemable at
Barnes & Noble. Limit one coupon per purchase. Valid in the U.S.A. and Canada only.

52614662

Canadian Retailers: Harlequin Enterprises Limited will pay the face value of this coupon plus 10.25¢ if submitted by customer for this product only. Any other use constitutes fraud. Coupon is nonassignable. Void if taxed, prohibited or restricted by law. Consumer must pay any government taxes. Void if copied. Inmar Promotional Services ("IPS") customers submit coupons and proof of sales to Harlequin Enterprises Limited, P.O. Box 3000, Saint John, NB E2L 4L3, Canada. Non-IPS retailer—for reimbursement submit coupons and proof of sales directly to Harlequin Enterprises Limited, Retail Marketing Department, 225 Duncan Mill Rd., Don Mills, ON M3B 3K9, Canada.

U.S. Retailers: Harlequin Enterprises Limited will pay the face value of this coupon plus 8¢ if submitted by customer for this product only. Any other use constitutes fraud. Coupon is nonassignable. Void if taxed, prohibited or restricted by law. Consumer must pay any government taxes. Void if copied. For reimbursement submit coupons and proof of sales directly to Harlequin Enterprises, Ltd 482, NCH Marketing Services, P.O. Box 880001, El Paso, TX 88588-0001, U.S.A. Cash value 1/100 cents.

5 65373 00076 2   (8100)0 12267

® and ™ are trademarks owned and used by the trademark owner and/or its licensee.

© 2017 Harlequin Enterprises Limited

MCOUPBN0617